Leah
A love story

Lois N. Erickson

REVIEW AND HERALD® PUBLISHING ASSOCIATION
HAGERSTOWN, MD 21740

Bible texts credited to RSV are from the Revised Standard Version of the Bible, copyrighted 1946, 1952, 1971, 1973.

R&H Cataloging Service

Erickson, Lois Nordling, 1920–
    Leah, a love story

    I. Title.

        [221.924]

ISBN 0-8280-0654-7

Other books by Lois N. Erickson
Adventures in Solitude
Huldah
Zipporah

Chapter 1

P ay the grain merchant," the young woman instructed the slave girl standing behind her. The merchant bowed respectfully. "I am grateful to you, Leah, daughter of Laban." Avoiding her eyes, he allowed his gaze to follow the curve of her shoulder and down the length of the brown-and-white robe that covered her youthfully rounded figure.

The slave girl stepped from behind her mistress. She reached into the pouch she carried and brought out proper payment. The merchant raised his head and extended his open hand to receive a piece of silver.

Both the merchant and Leah knew the price was fair. After several minutes of arguing over the cost for a basket of wheat, they had come to agreement. They recognized also that after the seller weighed the silver and dropped payment safely into his pouch, the buyer held the right to the last word.

Leah directed in her most businesslike voice, "Have your servant ready to carry the wheat to my donkey as soon as I finish my shopping."

"Yes, Mistress Leah. I'll do as you ask." The merchant bowed again.

"Come, Zilpah," she said to the maidservant. "We have other merchants to see." As she tilted her head proudly, her light-brown hair cascaded down her back to below her waist. A blue linen headscarf restrained it from falling across her face and into her light-brown eyes.

She turned away from the grain merchant's stall crowded between a seller of dates on one side and a spice merchant on the other. The stalls shared mud-brick walls, and woven reed mats roofed each one.

Zilpah followed, and they eased into the stream of shoppers

that crowded Haran's food market, leaving behind the aromas of dry grain, spicy cinnamon, and pungent marjoram. The servant girl balanced a basket crammed with dried figs and almonds on her head.

"You were smart with the bargaining, Mistress. Your father should have heard you today. He would have been proud of your getting the right price for the wheat."

"I did get a good price, didn't I?" Leah answered. She felt satisfied with her efforts. "Father is the one who taught me how to bargain. Of course, he's the best there is."

"You're just as good as he is at bargaining," the slave girl said. Then she added in a teasing tone, "Are we stopping anywhere else?"

"You know we're stopping somewhere else."

"For example, at the wool merchant's shop?"

They both giggled—the mistress and the slave—close in age, understanding each other's thoughts. Leah at 17 was only a year older than the servant. From the time they were small children, each had sensed the needs and desires of the other.

In the narrow passageway between the rows of stalls they pushed through the milling shoppers, avoiding those who stood solidly in front of the merchants, their voices raised in noisy haggling.

They left the food market area with its hard-packed dirt paths and turned onto a street paved with stone blocks. Although the street was narrow, the shops were larger than the food stalls. The business establishments shared tan mud-brick walls, but each also possessed a dome-shaped brick roof.

The dull sound of a wooden mallet on copper came from the coppersmith's shop. A maker of musical instruments drew his fingers across the strings of a lyre and the notes vibrated into the street. Fragrance of nard, heavily sweet and aromatic, drew Leah to a perfume shop. The merchant rubbed a bit of the oily scent on her hand, and she sniffed at it appreciatively. After bargaining, she nodded to Zilpah to pay the merchant for a small, ivory bottle of the perfume.

As they turned to leave, a dog darted in front of Leah and she stumbled into it. The servant girl grabbed her arm to keep her from falling.

"Why am I so clumsy?" Leah asked in exasperation. "I didn't see that dog at all."

4

"I would stumble too if a dog ran into me," Zilpah consoled her.

Leah partially closed her eyes, protecting them against the bright spring sunshine. She squinted ahead through the crowd of people. "We're almost to Teshar's shop. I hope he didn't see me stumble. I hope he was looking the other way."

"I can see him in his shop," Zilpah reported. "He's showing a length of cloth to a customer."

"Good," Leah replied with a relieved sigh. "Then probably he didn't see me almost fall down."

In contrast to the grain merchant's stall with his baskets of wheat and barley sitting on the dirt floor, the wool merchant Teshar had built a brick platform inside his shop and covered it with brightly colored woven rugs. Each morning he laid out woolen skeins spun from shades of red, brown, and black goat wool and creamy-white sheep wool. Folded bolts of woolen cloth rested on the rugs next to the skeins.

Leah and her maidservant stopped in front of the colorful display. The unmistakable smell of sheep and goat wool hovered in the air. The customer in the shop fingered a piece of red cloth one last time before handing over payment into Teshar's waiting hand. The wool merchant dropped the silver into his pouch and bowed to the departing customer.

Teshar was a slender young man, unlike the sturdy shepherds who worked for Leah's father. His black beard and neatly combed hair shone with a fragrant mixture of sesame oil and myrrh. He smelled different from the shepherds—they with the odor of sweat and sheep dung, he with the sweetly scented oil from his beard and hair mixed with the clean aroma of the washed wool he offered for sale. His person reflected the orderliness of his shop. Even when he strode across the fields each spring to buy wool from her father Laban, his bearing displayed that same orderliness.

Now without hesitating, Teshar stepped to the open front of his shop. "Welcome to my poor establishment." He smiled at her. "Come and rest on this humble man's rug." His voice did not match his words, however. It rang with the confidence of the successful wool merchant.

Leah sat down on one of Teshar's rugs. She carefully tucked her feet in their sheepskin boots under her long robe and pushed an escaping strand of her brown hair back under her head scarf. Standing with downcast eyes as if she were not planning to listen to the conversation, Zilpah waited courteously outside the shop. Her long black hair fell to the sides of her face, shadowing her large, slightly slanted Egyptian eyes.

Teshar took a seat near Leah. "And how is the lady of Master Laban's household today?" he asked as he smoothed a length of woolen cloth with his long, tapered fingers.

"I'm not the lady of the household," she protested. "You know I'm Laban's daughter."

"Of course. But I understand you have managed the household all these years since your mother died. Weren't you just a little girl then?" His voice revealed more interest in her than if she were just another customer. "I've heard that you manage well. The slaves obey. The food is well prepared. You have even raised your younger sister Rachel as if she were your daughter."

"How do you know all this?" she asked in surprise.

"Ah-ha!" he exclaimed. "I have my ways." His teeth flashed white in his dark beard.

Leah felt a flush rising from her neck. It continued up her face and into her scalp, and she hoped Teshar would not notice. She was unaccustomed to a man's compliments. He had gone to the trouble of finding out all about her, and she wondered what it could mean. Did she dare to hope he might have an interest in her—Laban's plainer daughter?

Confused, she lacked the courage to face him, and riveted her attention on his slender hands. A desire to touch them swept over her, but she resisted it. To have done so would have been improper.

She shifted her position on the rug and slid slightly away from him. "How—how," she stammered, "how is your mother?"

"Same as usual. Busy in the house, preparing my favorite foods, pushing the lazy slaves to do their work," he said lightly.

"And your four sisters?"

As usual also, sitting at the looms to weave the cloth I sell. This is fine wool that I buy from your father. Do you wish any of the yarn skeins today? I know you weave your own cloth."

"I need two more skeins of brown for the robe I'm weaving for my father," she answered. "Zilpah will pay you the price we agreed on last time I was in your shop." She hesitated a moment, wondering what else she could say. Shyly she asked, "Shall I give my father your regards?"

"Please give him my regards and give him a message."

"A message?"

"Yes, tell him I'll visit him this evening. I have business to discuss with him."

Once again he was the wool merchant, but he reached for her elbow to help her to her feet. She leaned into the strength of his grip, wishing he would never let go. He ran his hand down the sleeve of her robe, and then slid it over her hand, lingering briefly with his fingers on hers.

For a moment Leah remained speechless. Then her father's training rescued her.

"I shall prepare refreshments for your evening visit with my father." After a slight bow she stepped off the platform and into the narrow street.

Zilpah paid the wool merchant, and Teshar handed her two skeins of brown wool. Then the servant girl followed Leah into the street. "We mustn't forget the wheat you bought, Mistress," she reminded her as they threaded their way through the crowd.

"The wheat? Oh, yes, the wheat for the bread." After a pause she asked, "Did you hear what Teshar said?"

"I heard everything, every exciting, wonderful thing."

They turned back toward the food market and the reeking enclosure where they had left the donkey.

Zilpah dropped some almonds into the waiting hands of the urchin who had watched the animal while Leah did her shopping. He dashed away to the grain merchant to inform him that Mistress Leah was waiting. A husky slave brought the wheat and poured it into baskets slung on each side of the dark gray donkey.

With a smile Leah remarked to Zilpah, "We have everything we came for."

Zilpah nodded.

Stepping carefully to avoid fresh donkey dung, they left the damp dirt of the enclosure. Leah drove the donkey in front of her, using a willow whip to nudge it along. Zilpah followed with her basket, heavily laden with figs and almonds, on her head.

The narrow street led them past the sacred temple of the Sumerian moon god Sin. A solid, flat-tipped, man-made structure, 200 feet at the base and nearly 300 feet high, it rose splendidly above the flat surface of Haran. Three stairways on the tiered sides of the tan brick, pyramidlike tower led to the summit where a jeweled house crowned the peak. The opaque blue lapis lazuli and lustrous ruby-colored carnelian on the sides of the building glistened in the afternoon sun.

The great Sumerian king Ur-Nammu had built the sacred complex hundreds of years before. Even though Haran was a fortified, walled city, he had conquered it and other territories, claiming himself not only king of Ur and Haran but king of the four quarters of the world.

As they skirted the edge of the tower, Leah and Zilpah could hear the priests of the moon god chanting their prayers in the strange Sumerian language. Then the young women turned toward the section of the city where Leah's father, Laban, the sheepman, provided a home for himself, his daughters, and his household slaves.

"Open the gate, Narum," Zilpah shouted to the old slave who sat at the arched outer gateway to Laban's courtyard. Stiffly he got up to push open the wooden doors. Taking the willow whip from Leah, he drove the donkey across the courtyard and through an opening into a smaller, walled space.

Standing in the middle of her father's courtyard, Leah pointed to the mud-brick floor. "I want this swept and cleaned," she said to Zilpah and the other slave girl Bilhah. "The sun is already halfway down toward the horizon so you haven't much time."

What else should she have them clean? She surveyed her surroundings—the high brick wall that protected the courtyard and house from the street . . . the slightly lower wall that fenced off the enclosure for her father's two household donkeys and a milk goat. The old slave Narum also lived there in a hut with his 14-year-old grandson Gamesh.

Leah considered the rooms of the house, each with a door that led into the main courtyard. Tan burnt-brick walls formed square chambers with a domed brick roof rising above each room. Dark asphalt bitumen held the bricks in place.

To her right the first room held provisions—wheat, barley, millet, wine, oil, dates, and dried herbs. It served also as a protected food preparation center when cold winds blew down from the northern mountains.

Adjoining the storage chamber, a smaller room housed the two maidservants, Zilpah and Bilhah. Leah shared the next room, a larger one, with her sister, Rachel. Straight ahead of her she looked directly into the final room. Separate and situated at an angle from the others, it was her father's.

"When you have finished with the courtyard," she told the maids, "clean Master Laban's room."

Leah took dried figs from the basket that Zilpah had carried home. The outdoor food preparation table held the implements she needed—a flint knife to slice figs and chop almonds, a clay pot in which to cook them. Her hands moved quickly and surely, actions born of long practice. As she placed the sliced figs and an equal amount of water into the pot, her younger sister, Rachel, breezed into the courtyard from the street.

"Father's sheep are all watered and back at the shepherds' camp. I'm free for the rest of the day." Her slim young body spun around in a circle dance, barely missing Zilpah and Bilhah who were sweeping the bricks. Long dark hair swirled out behind her, and the bracelets on her ankles tinkled an accompaniment to her dance.

She stopped suddenly. "What's happening?" she asked. "Why are Bilhah and Zilpah cleaning everything?"

Leah chopped vigorously on the shelled almonds. "I'm waiting for Father to come home so I can tell him that he's having a guest."

"A guest, a guest!" Rachel sang as she whirled around the courtyard again. "You must think this guest is someone special." Stopping next to the table, she grabbed a handful of shelled almonds.

"Take the unshelled ones," Leah ordered. "I don't need to shell them for you."

"Yes, you should shell them for me. I've been working all day taking care of Father's sheep. You ought to shell almonds for me."

"Leave the almonds alone."

"All right, all right, but tell me who's coming."

Leah hesitated. Teshar's visit was no secret. Rachel could easily find out from the servants. Yet Leah hesitated. She suddenly felt reluctant to share the news with her more attractive sister. Deliberately she added honey and handfuls of chopped almonds to the figs and water, then carried the pot to the cooking fire.

"Well, answer me. Who is it?"

"The wool merchant Teshar."

"Handsome, rich Teshar, the seller of fine woolen cloth." Rachel circled in another enthusiastic round of dancing. "Won-

9

derful wool merchant Teshar, the man my unmarried sister hopes to marry."

"Stop it, Rachel! You don't know what you're saying."

"Yes, I do. I've been with you to the market and I've seen the way you act when you're around him."

Leah stirred the fig-and-almond mixture. Her sister's teasing voice grated on her already tense nerves. "He's probably coming to talk to Father about buying wool."

"You mean handsome, rich, wool merchant Teshar would bargain before he sees the wool at shearing time?" Rachel teased.

"And you're not to flirt with him like you do when we go to market."

"Who, me? Would I flirt with handsome, rich—?"

"Be quiet!"

"Don't tell me what to do. You're not my mother. I'll flirt if I want to." She flung herself across the courtyard and into the chamber the sisters shared.

By evening old Narum had barred the courtyard gate that led to the street. He sat leaning against the inside wall, waiting for the visitor.

That morning he had driven one of the donkeys to the food market to bring home a large skin of wine Laban had ordered. Narum had lingered in the marketplace to listen for any gossip he could report to his master—any gossip about their neighbors or about Laban's family.

Later he had sat at the doorway to his mud-brick, reed-roofed hut in the yard where he kept the donkeys. He needed to oversee his grandson as the boy hacked at piles of brush for Leah's cooking fire. Zilpah and Bilhah gathered the brush, but Gamesh cut it to the required length.

During the afternoon Narum had squatted outside the courtyard gate, observing who passed so he could report to Laban. Now, comfortably warm in his woolen robe, the old slave dozed. From long habit he could wake up at the slightest sound to open the gate.

Footsteps in the street roused him. He held a lighted torch and called through the cedar doors, "Who?"

"Teshar, the wool merchant."

The old man unbarred the gate. "Welcome to the house of Laban, Master Teshar." He bowed to the wool merchant. "I'll take you to Master Laban's room." Still holding the torch, he led the way across the quiet courtyard.

Laban sat cross-legged on a thickly woven carpet in his room, facing the door, waiting for his guest. He squared his broad shoulders and smoothed his graying beard. Then he leaned back casually against a pile of plump bolsters and pillows, all embroidered in rich shades of blue, red, and yellow. In the center of the room a brazier set on a tripod gave warmth. Orange coals glowed and smoke rose to escape through a hold in the center of the ceiling. Along a side wall baskets held Laban's clothes and personal possessions. Soft white sheepskins and woven robes formed a sleeping place. Behind him on a low, mud-brick shelf small bronze figures—his household gods—stood silently in a row. Oil lamps set on brick shelves provided shadowy light.

"Master Laban," called the old slave at the open door, "the wool merchant has arrived."

"Welcome to my modest home, Teshar," Laban said without getting up. "Enter and seat yourself."

"Thank you, Laban." He settled himself on a rug near another pile of cushions.

"Leah," Laban shouted into the air. "Bring refreshments." Then looking at the merchant, he added, "My daughter will serve us."

The visitor smiled and nodded.

Leah had waited in her room for her father's order. Now she hurried into the courtyard, Rachel following. Both of them had bathed and put on their prettiest robes—Leah's a creamy-white sheep's wool with blue geometric patterned embroidery at the neck, Rachel's a red goat's wool with yellow stripes woven into the sleeves.

Leah poured fermented sheep's milk into bowls and spooned the sweet fig-almond confection into a large dish.

"I'll serve the figs,' Rachel said, grabbing the dish.

"Wait!" Leah warned. "You know it's proper to serve the milk first." She scooted past her sister to the door of their father's room. There she waited dutifully until Laban commanded, "Bring the milk in, daughter."

Careful to avoid stumbling, she stepped across the threshold. She placed the two bowls in front of her father and then stood respectfully aside. Unconsciously she rubbed the back of her hand where Teshar had let his slender fingers linger for a brief

11

moment in his shop that afternoon.

Laban handed a bowl of milk to him. "Drink of my humble refreshment."

"You are very kind."

"And how is business at your shop?" the older man asked politely.

Leah didn't hear the answer. Her attention centered on her sister who waited impatiently at the door until their father said, "Bring in what you are carrying, girl."

Rachel flounced in with the fig confection and smiled at the visitor as she set the dish in front of her father. Before she turned away, she stepped slightly closer to Teshar, shrugged her shoulders, and ran her fingers through her long, dark hair.

Laban frowned at Rachel and motioned her away from his guest. "Bring more milk."

The girls went out. Twice more Leah brought milk, and then she and Rachel went to their room. Only later would they know the outcome of the conversation between the men.

"You honor me with a visit to my modest home," Laban began.

"The honor is mine," Teshar answered, "Because I have come to ask a favor."

"Ask your favor. Whatever I have is yours." Laban gave the polite reply.

"As you know," the younger man continued, "I have never taken a wife. I have my mother and four sister to support. Now my business is flourishing and I can easily support a wife as well as my mother and sisters."

"A wise decision, Teshar. A man needs a wife to give him sons."

Teshar paused to drink from his bowl of milk. Slowly he dipped two fingers into the dish of figs and lifted the sweet confection to his mouth. "You have two daughters," he observed.

Just as slowly Laban took some of the fig-almond mixture and chewed it before he answered, "Yes, I have two daughters."

"I have saved a generous bride-price so I am free to ask for one of them."

Laban smiled. "You honor me by asking for my daughter. She will make a good wife for you. She knows how to manage a household and can control the slaves. She knows how to cook, and is well into child-bearing age."

The merchant held up his hand to stop the other man from saying more. "A moment, please. I haven't come to ask for your older daughter. I have come to ask for the younger one, Rachel."

His host sat in stunned silence. Then he shifted uneasily against the cushions. "Why are you asking for the younger? You know it's traditional for the older daughter to marry first."

Teshar leaned forward. "I realize I'm going against the custom when I ask for the younger. Your older daughter has many abilities, and I considered the possibility of asking for her. But I already have a mother and four sisters who take care of my household. I'm sure you can find a good husband for her soon. I want to marry your younger daughter. I'm suitable. I have a good business. I can support her and many sons with all the luxuries they will need or want."

Sitting up straight, Laban folded his arms across his chest. "You have distressed me by asking for the younger before the older is married," he said firmly. "It's not the custom. I could never consider it."

"Then my visit is at an end. I will look elsewhere for a wife." Abruptly Teshar stood and stared down at Laban. "My thanks for your hospitality," he said in a cold, formal voice, then stalked out of the room. Laban could hear the street gate open and close.

In their room Leah and Rachel also heard it.

"What do you think they said to each other?" Rachel asked.

"I don't know," Leah answered, but her heart was sinking. "Their voices sounded angry just before Teshar left."

They looked out the door. Their father stood in the middle of the courtyard, his shoulders drooped. "There will be no marriage between our family and Teshar's," he said to his daughters. "Imagine a mere wool merchant asking for the younger daughter before the older."

Chapter 2

L eah, Leah!" Rachel's excited voice came from outside the
courtyard wall.

Leah looked up from the flat wheat bread she was
baking on top of the outdoor stone oven. She watched Rachel
run into the enclosed courtyard. As usual, she marveled at the
sight of the graceful girl. Rachel's dark hair spilled over her
slender shoulders while a red headband held it from falling
across her face. Her deep-set brown eyes always sparkled when
she brought some new discovery or exciting experience to share.

"What is it, child?"

"Don't call me 'child.' Can't you see that I'm grown up
now?" Rachel straightened her shoulders to emphasize the
budding figure under her yellow-and-red robe. "I'm 13 years old
already—old enough for a certain wool merchant to ask for me
in marriage."

Leaning over the hot stones of the oven, Leah squinted at the
baking bread. Rachel's words stung. She didn't want to think
about Teshar. For two weeks she had tried unsuccessfully to
forget the evening when he had asked her father for her younger
sister instead of for her.

With effort she controlled her voice. "I'm sorry, Rachel.
What do you want to tell me?"

"Exciting news. I was bringing Father's sheep to the well.
Some of the shepherds were already there. Then I saw a strange
man. He was arguing with the shepherds, and I heard him ask,
'Why don't you water the sheep and take them to pasture?' "

"He must be new around here if he doesn't know that the
shepherds wait until they're all at the well so they can roll the
cover off together."

"He is new. Wait till you hear what he did next." Her voice

mounted in enthusiasm. "When I brought Father's flock to the well, the man rolled the stone off all by himself."

"He must be strong!"

"But that's not the important part. He told me he's our cousin. He's Aunt Rebekah's son from Beersheba in the land of Canaan and has traveled all the way up here to Haran. He's our cousin Jacob."

"Our cousin Jacob! Are you sure?" Leah's hand paused in midair above the baking bread.

"Of course I'm sure. And, Leah, he's so good-looking. A real man, not just a shepherd boy. Where's Father? I want to tell him right away."

"He's in the house."

The girl dashed past her and through the door to their father's room.

Automatically Leah continued her task. She removed the baked bread from the stones and then reached into a stone mortar and lifted out ground wheat flour to make more dough. Dropping the flour into an earthenware bowl, she sprinkled a pinch of salt in it. Adding warm water—a small amount at a time—from a clay jar, she kneaded the mixture into a soft dough.

A kinsman. Aunt Rebekah's son. Our cousin Jacob.

Leah had never seen her father's sister. The woman lived hundreds of miles to the southwest. Strange rivers and unknown mountains and desert plains lay between Haran and Aunt Rebekah's home at Beersheba in Canaan. Many years ago Rebekah had gone there from this very house in Haran to marry her cousin, a man named Isaac.

Caravan leaders, traveling northeast, brought news from Beersheba to Haran. Years ago, before the birth of Leah and Rachel, Aunt Rebekah sent word to her brother Laban that she had presented her husband Isaac with twin sons, Esau and Jacob.

As the years passed, word came that the boys were well. Esau, they said, loved to hunt wild game. Jacob, however, preferred to work with his father's sheep and goats. Eventually Esau had caused his parents much grief by taking two women from the Hittite tribe for his wives. Jacob, though, remained unmarried.

Often Leah wondered how Rebekah had decided to leave Haran and go to Canaan. Leah glanced around the pleasant

15

courtyard and at the rooms, all domed like a collection of oversized beehives. She appreciated the home that her father provided.

The average residence in Haran had two rooms, one for men and one for women, and sometimes a small adjoining hut for a storeroom. Poorer families crowded into one room with only a woven cloth to divide the space for men on one side and women on the other. The poorest lived outside the city walls in small huts made from reed mats arched over a frame of bundled palm fronds.

Because of his keen business skills, her father could afford a comfortable home. His flocks were not as large as those of some other sheepmen, but he cared well for his animals, taking them to the best pastures—north in the summer, south in the winter. Neglected or poorly fed sheep produced uneven, coarse wool. It was weak with little elasticity. Her father's sheep grew strong, fine wool with good length to the fiber. The merchants called it fat wool for its excellent lanolin content. The fibers were oily with a protective film. His goats had equally good wool and their hair was resilient.

And her father knew how to bargain.

Leah loved her home. Outside the city walls down by the Balikh River, date palms swayed in the breezes. Vineyards stretched west across the plain. Farmland to the south yielded crops of onions, cucumbers, wheat, millet, and barley. Beyond the farmland her father pastured his flocks of sheep and goats.

The courtyard held beauty too. She would spare precious water for the fragrant oleander bushes that blossomed pink each season. A fig tree with its healthy green leaves stood in a sunny corner.

She cherished the herbs that thrived in her garden behind her father's room—mint, coriander, thyme, and large gray-green aloe plants.

Leah took a small portion of bread dough and rolled it into a ball between the palms of her hands. She placed it on a smooth, heavily floured stone and patted the ball to flatten it into a thin disk.

Would I, like Aunt Rebekah, be willing to leave Haran to marry a cousin? she pondered. *Or maybe to marry any man? I'm 17 already and Father hasn't found a husband for me yet. I'm years past the age when I should be promised in marriage. I'm so ashamed. And Father is disgraced because of me. Surely the idlers in the marketplace must say, "There goes the man with the homely, unmarried daughter."*

Turning the bread so it was well-floured on both sides, she slapped the flat disk of dough onto the hot stones over the fire.

And babies. I want to hold babies in my arms. I want to give Father grandsons to balance on his knees when he is old.

Sometimes when her father and Rachel were in the fields with the sheep and goats, Leah went alone to his room. There she would sit on a cushion by the low shelf where her father kept his household gods.

Some Teraphim were crude clay figures—but not her father's. His were made of bronze. He had bought them from the most skilled craftsmen. Their tiny faces showed fine detail. The goddess of love sat on a miniature chair of deep-blue lapis lazuli—that mysteriously opaque semiprecious stone. She held a baby to her breast.

Tenderly Leah would stroke the goddess of love and her child. She remembered how her mother had held the goddess and begged for a son. Once she had even carried the bronze figure to the sanctuary of the moon god Sin, and there on the man-made mountain among the blue and red stones had entreated the love goddess to send a son. How happy her mother had been when she found out that she expected a child!

Leah recalled the night of the baby's birth. The midwife came and gave expert care, but early in the morning before the sun's rays crept over the horizon both her mother and the baby boy lay dead. The memory was painful. *Why? Why had they died? What went wrong?* The goddess of love wanted women to have babies. It wasn't her fault.

Then Leah too would beg the goddess for a son but first, she knew, she needed a husband.

Now here was Aunt Rebekah's son. Cousin Jacob. Why had he come? Was he looking for a wife among his kinfolk?

She heard her father's footsteps as she strode out of the house and into the courtyard. "Make extra bread, Leah. We'll have a guest. A kinsman has arrived."

"Yes, Father." She watched him walk out the gate and into the street. He carried his tall frame proudly. Back straight. Feet firmly placed as he walked. His broad, strong shoulders showed the effect of many years of strenuous work among his flocks of sheep and goats. Strong lines marked his face, weathered from years of sun and rain and wind. His full gray beard, his piercing gray-brown eyes, and the firm set of his mouth gave the impression of a successful businessman. And so he was. Successful because he was shrewd, Leah knew.

A strong and intelligent man, her father. One of her greatest desires was to have strength of character and intelligence like his. Sometimes she wished she were his firstborn son instead of a 17-year-old daughter that no man wanted to marry. Of course, if she were a son, she couldn't give birth to children. But then, without a husband she couldn't have them anyway.

Rachel came into the courtyard from the house, her dark hair swinging loosely down her back. She danced over to Leah. "Father has gone to meet him."

"Yes, I know that Father has gone to meet him." She did not glance up from her baking.

"You don't sound very excited that our cousin Jacob has traveled all the way from Canaan."

Leah wiped the perspiration away from her forehead with the back of her hand. Earlier she had pulled her long brown hair into a thick braid that hung down her back and had covered her head with a scarf. Nervously she fingered it. "I don't like to meet strangers. They always stare at me because of my eyes. Men never notice my hands or my hair or anything nice about me. All they notice are my eyes."

"But, Leah, this man is our cousin. You must want to meet him."

"Why must I want to meet him?" Leah asked uneasily. "What does he look like?"

"Handsome. He's tall with strong shoulders—as big and broad as Father's, I'm sure. You should have seen the way he rolled the stone off the well. As I told you before, he's a real man, not just a shepherd boy to flirt with." Rachel giggled. Then she added knowingly, "I'll bet he's come to Haran to get a wife."

"What makes you so sure?"

"When I met him at the well, he kissed me."

Leah's heart sank. How could she ever compete with Rachel? Lively, sparkling, lovely Rachel. Jacob had already kissed the younger sister.

Rachel flitted over to the open gate to watch for their father and the kinsman. Sunshine splashed across her dark hair, giving it auburn highlights.

Leah touched her own light-brown hair. Would Jacob notice

that it was longer than Rachel's? She ran her hand down the side of her body. Would he see that her figure was more mature than her sister's?

"They're coming." Rachel's voice rose in excited anticipation. "I can see Father bringing him down the street."

In alarm Leah glanced from her sister to their room to the storeroom. The storeroom was closer. She dashed for the doorway. With her heart pounding, she hid behind a pile of empty baskets. Footsteps sounded on the courtyard bricks. Cautiously she peeked around the side of the baskets and out the doorway.

Her father and Jacob walked slowly across the courtyard toward Laban's room. It struck Leah how much they looked alike. They could have been father and son instead of uncle and nephew. Equally tall, they had the same wide shoulders; but Jacob's body was slimmer than his uncle's older, more mature frame. The main difference was the color of their hair and beards—Laban's gray, Jacob's dark brown.

Laban led the way to the house and entered his room. Leah could hear the deep rumble of her father's voice, and she knew he was offering the traditional words of hospitality, "Welcome, blessed of the Lord . . ."

Rachel dashed into the storeroom. "Did you see him, Leah? Did you see him?"

She stepped from behind her hiding place. "Yes, I saw him."

"Isn't he good-looking? Do you think he came to find a wife?"

"How should I know if he's after a wife?" At the hurt expression on her sister's face, Leah instantly regretted her brusque reply.

"Why are you angry with me?" Rachel asked.

"I'm sorry I sound angry. I'm not angry, I'm afraid. I mean, when Jacob sees me, I'm afraid he'll look the other way."

They heard their father summon the young slave Gamesh to bring a basin of water to wash the guest's feet.

"I need to get some milk," Leah said more to herself than to Rachel. Then she added, "Go back to the sheep, Rachel."

Her sister pouted. "I don't want to go."

"Take some bread to eat, and go." Putting her hand on the girl's back, Leah urged her through the door.

The milk was kept cool in a pit in a corner of the storeroom. Leah removed the wooden lid and briefly enjoyed the damp air that rose from it. She lifted out a jug of sheep's milk and smelled it to make sure it was properly fermented. Then she poured some into a pottery bowl.

She must take it to her father so he could offer the refreshment to their guest. First she tucked any loose strands of hair under her head scarf. Pausing at the doorway to her father's room, she took a keep breath to still the pounding of her heart. Then she stepped from the sunlit courtyard into the cool, dark interior of the room.

For a moment she could see only vague shapes.

"Bring it over here, Leah." Her father's voice directed her to where he sat cross-legged on a woolen rug. She handed the bowl to him, and he presented it to Jacob opposite him on a thick sheepskin.

"Drink, Nephew Jacob," he said. "Welcome to the food and drink in my home." Her father added the formal phrase reserved for kinfolk. "Surely you are my bone and my flesh."

Leah stood behind her father, staring at her feet. Then the temptation proved too great, and she glanced over her father's gray head at the man. She could see his dark-brown hair and beard, but the shadow in which he sat kept her from seeing his face, so she lowered her eyes again.

"How is your father Isaac?" Laban inquired.

Jacob answered in a guarded voice. "My father is very old. His eyesight is dim and now he spends most of his time in his tent. I oversee the shepherds he hired for his many flocks of sheep and goats." Pausing, he glanced down at his hand, then struck his right fist into the palm of his left hand. "My brother Esau cares little for the life of a shepherd. He prefers roaming the hills in search of wild game."

"And do you bring news of my sister Rebekah, your mother?"

"As you know, my mother is much younger than my father. She is still considered a beautiful woman."

"She was a beautiful young girl when she left Haran to marry your father Isaac, son of my uncle Abraham."

The conversation was polite. Custom dictated that three days must pass before Laban could even hint that he wished to know why Jacob had journeyed to Haran.

"I will want to learn more of your father and mother and brother," he continued. "First you must rest from your tiresome journey. Accept my hospitality for as long as you wish. Eat and drink well in my house. The maidservants will make a bed of sheepskins for you here in my room."

He turned toward Leah who was still standing behind him. "Bring more milk, daughter."

Twice more she brought bowls of fermented milk. She knew her father wanted to show proper hospitality. That meant presenting milk to the guest three times. Then she brought warm flat bread and boiled lentils fragrant with sweet onions and a touch of coriander.

Later when she came to pick up the bowls, her father had gone out. Jacob had fallen asleep on a thick rug, his head on a cushion. A compelling desire urged her closer. Furtively she tiptoed to his side. Light from the courtyard streamed through the doorway and fell across his face. She could see his full, dark beard. His dark-brown hair curled slightly.

He slept with an arm flung up so that his head rested on one of his large, strong hands. His robe sleeve had slipped back, revealing his muscular arm, brown from the sun. The red robe, woven with bands of white, was dirty and worn but of good quality, made from fine sheep and goat wool.

Warily Leah leaned down for a better view of his face. Rachel was right. He was a handsome man. The brown skin above his beard was smooth and unblemished. His closed eyes were deep-set, his brows full and masculine.

What she noticed most was that he slept in exhaustion. Why had he hurried across hundreds of miles between his home in Canaan and her father's house?

Unexpectedly he roused from sleep, flinging his right arm out in a gesture of defense. His hand struck her knee. Startled, she jumped back. Jacob's eyes flew open and he sprang to his feet. "I sensed that someone was watching me," he said sharply as he towered above her. "But I didn't mean to hit you. Why were you standing so close? Why are you in this room?"

Leah avoided his gaze. "I just came in to pick up the milk bowls."

"You were watching me. It's bad enough to endure that row of your father's idols looking at me without having his daughter staring, too."

She glanced toward the low shelf that held her father's gods. "Those aren't idols. They're my father's household gods." Her voice became firm and controlled. Laban would never back down from accusation, and she determined to imitate him. "And

I wasn't staring. I've never met a cousin before. I wanted to see how much you looked like our family."

"Family," he said in a low voice. He lay down on the rug again and closed his eyes. "I left my family in Beersheba. At times I thought I'd never make it all the way here to Haran. Rachel was a welcome sight when I saw her at the well."

A faint smile relaxed his face, and the frown on his forehead faded. "Of course, I have another reason for this visit with my uncle." He opened his eyes. His voice became stronger. "But I don't know why I'm telling you all this. I need to sleep now. Don't let anyone wake me up." Jacob paused to chuckle. "No one—unless it's Rachel."

Hastily Leah picked up the milk bowls.

Unless it's Rachel . . . unless it's Rachel. Always men noticed her. Already she had attracted Jacob.

Then in swift strides Leah returned to the cooking fire. She hit the bread dough with fierce strokes and slapped the round cakes onto the hot stones.

Chapter 3

Satisfied that his guest was resting comfortably, Laban left the courtyard. The sound of his leather sandals echoed off the city wall as he headed toward South Gate. The fortified wall, 30 feet high and 6 feet thick, towered above him. Laban approved of the security it gave the city in case of an invasion.

He had built his home inside the wall near South Gate. From the gate it was a short distance—an easy walk—to the pastureland.

South Gate was an arch built through the thick wall. Massive oak doors covered with bronze stood at the far side of the arch. The doors, strong and reliable, remained open during the day. Beyond the arch he proceeded along the road that ran past the city's farmlands. Spring wheat, a few inches high, tinted the fields green. Laban passed a brown, recently plowed section and then a field of barley. In the distance wooden waterwheels creaked as they lifted river water to irrigate the crops. The river's current turned the ingeniously designed wheels. Pottery jars, lashed along the rims, spilled water into an aqueduct that carried it to the fields.

A breeze from the east brought the fresh scent of green plants, the earthiness of newly turned soil, and the damp aroma of sunshine on irrigation water.

Laban looked neither to the right nor the left. Even though he noticed the beauty of the green fields, he had no desire to speak to a farmer. Sheepmen and farmers seldom spoke. They maintained a tenuous, uneasy truce. At times it broke when farmworkers attacked shepherds in retaliation for allowing sheep and goats to stray into the fields.

Glancing ahead to his flocks, he smiled. The sight of his sheep and goats always gave him a cheerful and prosperous feeling. Well cared for, productive, the animals were his security and his satisfaction.

Another smile crossed his face when he thought of the guest resting in his home. Jacob would make a fine husband for Leah. What more could a father hope for as a husband for his elder daughter than a kinsman and a sheepman? Jacob was both. Laban had no doubt his nephew and come to Haran to take a wife. Like Jacob's father Isaac, he wanted a wife from among his own people.

Often Laban had muttered to himself, "I refuse to be the father of an unmarried daughter." Yet he had failed so far in his efforts to find a husband for Leah. Now here was Jacob. Here was the man for her. As he walked, he worked out a plan in his mind. Tomorrow he would ask Jacob to help with shearing the sheep and goats. Surely within a week or two the kinsman would ask for Leah and Laban would agree to a marriage contract, after proper bargaining of course. He would arrange for the wedding feasts at the completion of shearing and before taking the flocks to summer pasture. No need to wait for a year's betrothal since Leah was already past marrying age. He stroked his beard and continued to smile.

A month later Laban was no longer smiling.

In the pasture he watched his nephew shear a sheep. No doubt about it, the man knew how to handle the flint shearing knife. Jacob crouched over the sheep, holding the animal firmly between his knees. He had laid aside his robe and now wore only his sandals and a short garment girded securely around his hips. In the warm spring sunshine his bare shoulders and back muscles tensed. He grasped the shearing knife firmly and with a practiced hand he cut wool from the ewe.

A valuable shepherd this visitor from Canaan. But impolite! He had been in Haran a month already and still hadn't explained why he had come. Didn't he know that three days was the traditional and proper time allowed before a visitor should tell his mission?

Laban's fingers fidgeted with the thick hair on his upper lip. Two problems troubled his mind. Leah must have a husband — this was his main concern. Jacob was the logical solution to his problem, but his nephew hadn't asked for her.

The other problem was the bride-price. Could Jacob pay? He had arrived in Haran with only a small pack. It was large enough, however, to carry sufficient gold; but in the time that Jacob had lived in the house, Laban had seen no gold, no silver. At least this problem was less serious. Jacob was a skilled shepherd, and a man of his abilities could work out a bride-price.

The time had come to find out more about the intentions of the kinsman from Canaan.

Laban watched as the shearing continued, the wool rolling neatly off the sheep. The ewe scrambled to her feet and ran back to her lamb in the nearby flock. Finally Laban strolled over to where Jacob squatted on the ground, examining the wool.

"You have worked hard today. Rest awhile," he said, taking a position opposite Jacob. He would open the conversation and guide it cautiously until he got the information he wanted. "You have been here a month already. It's good you arrived in time for shearing. That's when I need extra help."

"Shearing is the best time of the year," Jacob replied pleasantly. With his fingers he combed wisps of wool out of his dark-brown beard. Slipping his hands into the fleece again, he tested its resilience. "This month has passed quickly. Time always passes quickly when I work with the sheep."

The older man picked up a piece of the fleece and squeezed it in his hand. The fibers were long and oily—top quality. "I can see that you know the business. Of course, you told me before that your father has large flocks."

"Yes, my father owns large numbers of animals—sheep, goats, donkeys, and camels." Jacob's voice was steady. "He pastures them over wide areas near Beersheba."

Guarding against any direct show of probing for information, Laban commented casually, "He taught you how to shear, but now you are not there to help him at shearing time."

"He owns slaves and he hires many shepherds. Even my brother Esau helps at shearing time."

Laban glanced away as anger swept over him. He was giving Jacob every opportunity to explain his reasons for journeying to Haran and how long he planned to stay. Yet this younger man—his own sister's son—remained discourteous. Jacob was forcing him to become impolite. Now he would have to question him directly.

As Laban stood up, his nephew rose also. Their eyes met, Jacob's on a level with his. The thought flickered in Laban's mind, *A man to watch, not to trust completely.*

"For the past month you have served me for only a place to sleep and for food to eat. I could hire you and give you wages. What would you consider fair wages?"

"I'm satisfied to work with the sheep and goats." The kinsman continued to withhold the information Laban wanted. "Wages are not important."

"No matter how long you stay, I'm willing to give you pay for your work," his uncle offered as he probed for an answer.

"I would work for three years without wages."

At last Jacob was giving some information. He expected to stay at least three years. How long before he would tell why he had come and what wages he expected? Laban chose his next words carefully. "My home is your home. Stay with me."

"I will stay," Jacob replied solemnly. Then he shrugged and lifted his hands. "What do wages matter to me?"

Laban sensed that Jacob was ready to tell what he wanted. He waited. After a moment's hesitation his nephew said, "You have two daughters."

"Yes, I have two daughters."

"I know it's the custom for a man to pay a bride-price. As you know, I traveled with a light pack when I came from Canaan. The journey was long and I used my silver and gold along the way."

His face impassive Laban shrugged. "What does a bride-price matter?" He paused to allow the younger man to save face to make the offer. They both knew the importance of the bride-price for a marriage contract.

"I'm an experienced shepherd." Jacob spoke quietly, firmly. "I know the business. If I work for you, your flocks will increase. I will work for you to pay the bride-price."

Stroking his beard, the gesture that would indicate the honesty of his words, Laban prompted, "For one of my daughters."

Jacob put his hand on his own beard. "I will serve you three years for your younger daughter, Rachel."

So! He had come to find a wife among his relatives, but he hadn't asked for the older daughter. The proper request would have been to request Leah. Jacob, his own kinsman, was just as impolite as the wool merchant Teshar. Laban pressed his lips together to keep from shouting at his nephew. Hadn't Jacob's mother taught him any manners? *He wanted the younger daughter*. But then, who could blame him?

Of course he would desire Rachel—graceful, lovely Rachel. No man would prefer the plainer Leah.

"Three years?" Laban replied. "You're offering only three years for my daughter Rachel? Ten years of labor would be a fairer price for that beautiful young girl."

"Ten years! How can a man wait that long for his bride? I'm not going to wait that long." Jacob paused, then offered, "I would give serious thought to five years for Rachel."

"Five years! I might consider letting my older daughter Leah go after five years. In Haran it's the custom for the older daughter to marry first. But I would never release my younger daughter for less than seven years."

"I'm from Canaan. Is it necessary to follow all of your customs?" Jacob stared at the ground. "Seven years for Rachel, you say? That's too long." He raised his head and met Laban's gaze. "But I agree to seven years because you are my mother's brother."

"Since you are my sister's son, it's better that I give my daughter to you than to any other man. I agree to seven years."

So be it, Laban thought. He would have seven years of Jacob's skill with the flocks, and he would have that long to find a husband for Leah. Never would he allow anyone to marry his younger daughter before he found a husband for the older one.

"Do we need witnesses for the agreement?" Jacob asked.

They looked at each other for a moment in silence.

So he distrusts me as much as I distrust him, Laban mused. *And now he has insulted me by asking for witnesses. I will save my honor by agreeing.*

"Because we are of the same family, we know we don't need witnesses," Laban replied, "yet it's the custom here in Haran to make a formal agreement with the aid of them."

"When shall we make this formal agreement?"

"When I complete the shearing. At that time I prepare a feast for the wool merchants and the shepherds. At the feast I'll call in witnesses."

"I can wait till then." Jacob stooped to pick up the shearing knife. Laban watched him return to the flock and choose another ewe to shear.

But the older man's anger still burned. He had agreed to high wages for Jacob—his beautiful daughter Rachel. Even further, he had promised to provide witnesses for the formal agreement. But then his anger started to subside as he once more realized that he had also gained seven years of hard work from an experienced and valuable sheepman. An excellent bride-price. A smile of satisfaction lurked at the corners of his mouth as he started toward the flock.

Across the pastureland he saw movement. Leah and a maidservant were bringing the midmorning meal.

Where could he find a husband for her? She was well developed and not bad looking in many ways. If a man didn't see her squint, he would consider her attractive with her long brown hair flowing from beneath her bright head scarf. She moved easily when she walked. Only occasionally did she stumble on a stone or stick in the path.

He knew she was intelligent and capable with good business abilities. If she were his firstborn son instead of a daughter, he would feel confident in giving her the birthright, the inheritance of all his sheep, goats, slaves, and other possessions.

Why had the gods afflicted him with an unwanted girl? Why, for that matter, two daughters and no sons? Laban sighed. When he had time, he would find a new wife to carry his seed and produce sons for him. No, he must make time soon. He needed sons. Maybe he could find a widow so he wouldn't have to put up with another young girl in the house.

Stooping, he ran his hand over the wool. Soft and warm under his fingers, it smelled of a good, healthy sheep. The feel and scent of the wool eased his agitation. A film of oil clung to his fingers. The wool was heavy and long this year, and the merchants paid a good price.

He looked across the field again at his older daughter and shook his head. His mouth set in determination. Once thing he was sure of—no man was going to marry Rachel before he found a husband for Leah. His daughters would marry in the proper order.

As Leah and Zilpah walked toward the shearing ground, Leah carried a cloth filled with barley loves in one hand and a goatskin of fermented milk over her shoulder. An earthen pot filled with warm boiled wheat and garlic balanced on Zilpah's head. She held a straw mat in one hand.

Leah felt her heart start to race. It often happened when she knew she would see Jacob. Halting, she squinted against the sunshine, trying to pick out his figure.

"Zilpah," she asked, "can you see Jacob?"

"He's over to the left near your father."

"Yes, now I see him."

Since that first day when Jacob had accused her of watching him, he had never mentioned the incident. One evening in the courtyard she had asked about Rebekah. After expressing his love and admiration for his mother, he remained with his head bowed for a long time. As he sat in silence, a surge of sympathy for his loneliness gripped Leah. She wanted to say, "If I were your wife, I could comfort you. Ask for me and I'll help you overcome your longing for your home."

But she was afraid. She remembered vividly how on that first day he had ordered her to leave him alone.

"Mistress Leah." Zilpah's voice brought her back from her thoughts.

"Yes, Zilpah?"

"Are you glad that Master Jacob came to Haran?"

Leah glanced sideways at the servant girl. "He's a help to Father."

Zilpah smiled broadly. "He's more than a good shepherd. I think he would make a good father for someone's children."

She giggled, and Zilpah laughed with her.

Leah loved to watch Jacob with the sheep. His strong hands were gentle, and the animals trusted him. She especially liked to observe him as he sheared. He moved with steady assurance. In half the time it took most shepherds, he had the wool removed, seldom drawing blood with a slip of the knife.

Now he faced away from her. She moved closer and to one side. His brown legs were bare. For a while she stared at the long, hard muscles of his calves and thighs, then pulled her gaze up from his legs to his brown shoulders. His body tensed with the effort he used as he clutched the shearing knife and sliced the wool.

Pulling her thoughts back to her duties, she spoke to Laban. "Father, I've brought the midday meal."

"Unpack it, girl. We're hungry and thirsty."

Zilpah laid the straw mat on the ground and placed the pot of boiled wheat and garlic on it. Leah set out the barley loaves and the goatskin of fermented milk.

The two men sat cross-legged on the ground next to the food. Tearing off bits of the bread, they used it to carry the thick boiled wheat to their mouths. Each took turns drinking milk from the goatskin. After the men wiped their hands on their bare legs and returned to the shearing, Rachel came to eat. Then Zilpah gathered the empty pot and depleted goatskin. As Leah picked up the straw mat, she glanced once more at Jacob. He was already shearing another ewe.

Laban watched the two young women hike across the pasture toward home. A sudden concern seized him. How would Leah react when she heard that he had promised her sister to Jacob? He had always said that he would not arrange marriage for the younger before the elder daughter. The news that he had given his promise for Rachel would devastate Leah. She would think he was disregarding her, showing no concern for her rights.

Leah, oh, Leah! Why was she his favorite child? Rachel, lively and beautiful, charmed all who met her. She charmed him too. But Leah—he loved her because she was strong and intelligent like himself. And although she was female, she was his firstborn. He would have to upset her now, but the time would come when he would show her that he had no intention of shoving her out of her rightful place.

Evening came and a sunset brought a cool west wind. In the courtyard Leah pounded dried coriander seeds to add to the garbanzo beans and garlic. The zesty aroma of the seeds rose from her stone mortar and pestle.

She could hear Rachel at the loom, working on strips for a new tent. They had moved one of the looms into the courtyard and set it near the north wall. Early spring sunshine warmed that side of the courtyard. Rachel slid the shuttle back and forth. Slowly she worked coarse black goat hair into the thick yarn strung on the loom. With a narrow wooden stick she beat the woven goat hair to make the cloth firm.

Zilpah removed a round of flat bread from a hot stone and dropped an unbaked one in its place. "Shall I light a torch, Mistress?" she asked Leah. "It's growing dark."

"Yes, light a torch. It's time those men came in to eat."

Shortly Leah heard their footsteps outside the wall, and then Jacob and her father entered the courtyard. The sounds from the loom stopped. Rachel watched Jacob walk across the courtyard and into the house.

"How many more days of shearing, Father?" Leah asked.

"Five. Do you have the tent ready for summer pasture?"

"I'll have the tent, provisions, donkeys, and servants ready to go." She knew they mustn't delay departure to summer pasture.

During the shearing, merchants came daily to buy wool and goat hair from her father. At the end of the shearing season he would host a feast for the businessmen and his workers. Then a few days later her father, Rachel, and she would set out toward the northern mountains with the caravan of sheep, goats, shepherds, slave men and women and children. They would reach the first of new pastureland after three days.

Leah wondered if Jacob would go with them.

Laban glanced toward his younger daughter seated by the loom. "Rachel, come here."

She dashed to her father and, rocking on tiptoes, smiled up at him expectantly.

He took hold of her arm. "Hold still. I have something to tell you." Raising his head, he called to Leah, "Come here, too. I want you to hear this at the same time."

She detected an unusual intensity in her father's voice. Only something of great importance would cause him to speak with that deep serious tone. What could it be?

Leah dropped the bread dough back into the earthenware bowl. With eyes wide and one hand over her mouth, she walked to her father. For some unknown reason she dreaded to hear what he was about to tell them.

Chapter 4

"I might as well let you know now," Laban said to his daughters, "I have promised Rachel to Jacob."

For a moment Rachel stood completely still. Then she hugged her father and kissed him high on his cheek above the beard, at the same time squealing with delight.

"Thank you. Thank you, Father, for promising me to Jacob."

Feeling as if someone had struck her, Leah backed away and sat down on a stool. Laban glanced down at her and bit his lip.

"When, Father, when?" Rachel asked.

"After seven years. He has to work out the bride-price first."

"But that's so long from now," the girl whined. "Couldn't you make it sooner?"

"No, I can't make it sooner." Turning, he entered the house.

Rachel ran to where Leah sat on the stool. "Did you hear, Leah? I'm promised to Jacob."

"I'm sure it's nice to be promised. But how could Father do that? I'm older. He's always said he would promise me first."

"There's still time for Father to find a husband for you. Jacob has to work out the bride-price. Seven years."

Rachel glided around the courtyard and circled back to her sister. "I know that Father prefers you. This time for a change he's doing something nice for me." She whirled away and disappeared into her room.

Leah felt Zilpah's hand on her shoulder. "Shall I bring another torch? Would you like more light?"

"It doesn't matter. I'm 17 already and I'm not married. I'm not even promised. No one wants me. I'm sure Jacob despises me."

Ten days later after the completion of the shearing and the merchants had bargained with Laban, he provided a generous feast. During it he signed the formal betrothal agreement.

Leah turned her efforts toward preparations for the trek north. "Rachel, stop daydreaming and come help pack." Her voice carried more than a hint of sharpness. She felt irritable and couldn't shake off the melancholy that had overcome her the evening she found out that their father had promised her sister to the visiting kinsman.

"I'm coming. You don't have to shout at me."

"Zilpah and I are packing bowls and pots. Here, take this saddlebag for Father's gods. Wrap them in cloth so they won't get scratched."

"I know how to pack father's gods. I've done it before." Rachel picked up the saddlebag and flounced into the house.

Leah pursed her lips. It was late afternoon on the final day before they departed. Why couldn't Rachel cooperate?

"Zilpah, did you send Narum and Gamesh to the shepherds' camp for extra donkeys?"

"Yes, Mistress. They should return any time now."

In the courtyard bags of provisions stood ready for the journey to summer pasture. Laban had ordered household preparations completed so his caravan could leave at daybreak the following morning. He depended upon Leah to make sure that all was ready.

"You can finish here," she said to the servant girl. "I need to pack some herbs."

She carried a pouch with her to the storeroom where covered pots held the aromatic herbs that she had harvested and dried. "Let me see. What do I need? Comfrey for sore muscles and wounds. Marjoram for toothache. Mint for stomach ailments." For cooking she added coriander seeds, salvia, and thyme.

She wrapped the herbs separately in pieces of linen cloth, tying each packet with yarn. Next she filled a small clay jar with a dull green salve—dried yarrow mixed with rendered sheep tallow.

With all the packets and the jar in her pouch, she went to her herb garden and pulled fresh aloe plants.

As she worked, she wondered where Jacob was—probably surpervising the other shepherds. He and her father would rest in a tent tonight. Leah wished she could stop thinking about him so often, but her mind returned constantly to him—Jacob shearing a sheep, Jacob drinking goat milk she brought to him, and her father's voice saying, "I've promised Rachel to Jacob."

By the time Zilpah had packed the last bowl, darkness dimmed the courtyard. Leah ached with fatigue. With a sigh of relief she left the courtyard and stumbled into her room.

She woke up at dawn. A bit of light from the ceiling hole and from the side wall ventilation slits blurred her vision. The sky had begun to lighten although the sun was still hidden below the horizon. She could barely see the tan, mud-brick walls of the room that extended upward to form a domed roof. The top bricks were blackened from fires she built in the brazier during cool days.

Then she heard Rachel's gentle breathing.

How young and innocent her sister was! Leah felt a pang of guilt that she had lost patience with her the last few days. Rachel couldn't help that she was pretty and Leah was plain.

Maybe she's the only child I'll ever raise, she pondered. *Maybe I'll never have any of my own.*

Leah pulled a brown-and-red robe over her cream-colored tunic. She tied on a pair of sturdy goat leather boots, good foot coverings for the rocky trail the caravan would follow to the north.

When she walked into the courtyard, her eyes slowly focused. She could see the morning sky, apricot-colored in the east.

Zilpah's voice came from the donkey enclosure. "Here, you donkey, stand still! Bilhah, come hold this animal while I tie on the saddlebags."

After opening the gate to the enclosure, Leah surveyed the scene with satisfaction. The maidservants were loading the donkeys with bags of household items—bowls and pots, rugs, pillows, sheepskins, and baskets of food. One donkey carried only the heavy goat-hair tent.

She knew that the main part of the caravan with her father's flocks was assembling in the fields. Soon they would move out toward summer pasture.

It was Leah's favorite time of the year, and she was eager to start the journey. Hurrying back through the courtyard and into her room, she grabbed an ivory comb to untangle her long hair.

"Get up, Rachel. It's time to go."

"I'm up, I'm up." The girl sat up and yawned, then reached for another comb.

Leah glanced around the room. Several months would pass before they would sleep in it again. She liked their father's house, but even better she enjoyed living in a tent.

She loved the freedom.

Freedom from the thick walls of the house with tiny slits for ventilation—slits that gave some protection from blowing dust but also let in too little light.

Freedom from the stares of people in the marketplace.

Freedom to wander among the trees and scuff through the grass in the meadows. The sheep and goats, instead of being pastured far from the house, fed on grass near the tents. There she would talk to the animals and run her hands over lambs and kid goats. She smiled when she thought of how she used to roll around on the grass with the baby animals when she was a child.

During summer pasture she liked to get up early and watch the sun rise from behind the rocky crests of the mountains. In the fall and winter she migrated with her father's caravan south along the river, but Leah preferred summer in the northern hills.

Zilpah's voice broke into her thoughts. "We've finished packing the donkeys and have them outside the gate."

In the street the animals waited impatiently for the signal to start. Leah gave last-minute instructions to the old slave Narum and his grandson Gamesh who would remain at the house.

"Come on, Rachel," she said. They closed the courtyard gate behind them.

Leah, Rachel, and the maidservants hurried the donkeys down the street toward the city gate. Just once Leah glanced back at the house. Only its beehive-shaped roofs showed above the courtyard wall.

Outside South Gate they drove the donkeys past fields of green wheat. With willow switches they kept the animals from running into the fields planted with new onions and cucumbers and away from the lush green wheat and barley. At last they came to the spreading pastureland where the main part of the caravan bustled in preparation. Shepherds' wives and children loaded goat-hair tents and sheepskins, food and pots onto the backs of more donkeys. After they finished packing, the women slung goatskin bags of milk over their own shoulders.

"Where's Jacob?" Leah whispered to Zilpah.

"He's on the far side of the field with some other shepherds. They're driving the sheep this way." The maidservant herded together a few of the shorthaired milk goats.

Leah circled her donkeys, trying to keep them in place. Whenever possible she squinted toward the approaching sheep, watching Jacob.

To the east the sun peeked above a distant hill. Its rays reached toward the milling animals and shepherds, suggesting too much heat before the end of the day.

At the head of the assembly Laban raised his hand.

"Ai! Ai!" the shepherds shouted at the animals. The ewes and rams answered in low-pitched tones, the lambs in high cries. The caravan started to move.

Summer pasture! Tingles of excitement ran through Leah's stomach.

Laban led his caravan in a long, narrow line past the fields of wheat and barley. Farm workers stood at intervals along the sides of the road, slingshots grasped in their hands, ready to attach any animal that might turn into the fields. *Or any shepherd,* thought Leah, remembering her father telling her that farmers and shepherds had been at enmity with each other since the beginning of time.

Leaving the farmland behind, Laban circled widely around Haran and then headed north along the west bank of the Balikh River, an easy, well-traveled route this first day with plenty of water for animals and people. Men herded the large flocks of sheep and goats, urging them along with their shepherd's sticks tipped with knobs of hard resin.

Using switches, Leah and the women kept the loaded donkeys and the milk goats moving. As they trekked across the gently rising plain, Leah often glanced ahead. She was glad when broad daylight came. Then it was easier to pick out Jacob's figure from among the shepherds. More often she saw her father. He shifted from one place to another, keeping a careful watch over his possessions as the flocks traveled steadily northward.

They passed villages huddled near the river. The huts, shaped like camel bells, consisted of rush mats arched over bundles of palm fronds. Near every village farmers rushed to the edges of their fields and shouted curses at Laban and his shepherds. Dogs barked furiously at the passing flocks.

Laban returned curse for curse to the farmers. He and his shepherds waved their slingshots high above their heads to show that they were armed against any attack by men or dogs.

In late afternoon the caravan halted for the night in a wide pasture. The animals spread out by the river and up the slopes of low hills.

Leah and Zilpah lifted the heavy tent from the donkey. Relieved of its burden, the animal rolled happily in the grass and then scrambled to its feet to start grazing.

Zilpah and Bilhah unloaded the other donkeys and then went to gather brush and dry sheep dung left from last year's migration for the cooking fire.

Rachel came to help put up the tent. A strong odor rose from the black goat-hair tent as Leah and Rachel laid it out. It reminded Leah of her own tent, folded and waiting in a storage shed. She had woven it from goat hair—black, brown, and red. One by one the lengthy strips had come off the loom. Later Zilpah sat on the brick floor and sewed them together with thick, strong yarn. Of course, with no husband Leah had never used her tent. It remained on the floor of the lean-to storage shed in the donkey enclosure. Next to it lay strips for Rachel's tent, the one she was still weaving.

Now Leah and Rachel raised their father's tent, using sticks the donkeys had carried. They hung partitions woven from sheep's wool to make a private space for themselves and the maidservants at one end and another for their father and Jacob at the other. The center of the tent remained open to the front and the back.

Rachel set the household gods on a rug in their father's end of the tent. The small bronze figures stood in a row—the fierce storm god standing on a panther, a little boy god wearing a long tunic, the shepherds' god with a staff in his hand (their father's favorite), the goddess of love sitting on her blue stone chair and nursing her baby.

Jacob lifted the side of the tent. He stopped abruptly and stared at the bronze figures. "I've endured these idols on a shelf in your father's house," he said firmly. "Now you have even brought them into the tent."

"Father would never leave his gods with just two servants to guard the house," Leah explained.

"The goddess of love is my favorite." Rachel stoked the bronze baby that the image held in its arms.

"Don't touch it!" Jacob shouted.

Rachel jumped away from the figurine.

The kinsman's voice was tense. "I don't want anything to harm you, Rachel. You mustn't worship them, nor you either,

Leah. You must worship only the Lord."

"Did you bring an image of him?" Rachel asked. "I want to see what he looks like."

"With the Lord you don't need an image."

"Do you mean that your father's household has only one god?" Leah inquired.

"There is only one God, the God of my grandfather Abraham and my father Isaac."

"I don't understand," Leah replied. "How can one god take care of shepherds and women and children and people in more than one city?"

"The Lord is all-powerful."

She paused for a moment. "Father worships these gods, but he worships the Lord, too," she told him.

"There is only one God and He is the Lord," Jacob insisted.

How can he be so sure? Leah questioned in her mind.

Jacob observed her hesitancy. "You may doubt what I say, Leah, but never doubt the goodness of the Lord."

As he turned to leave the tent, he almost collided with their father. "Leah, come quickly," Laban called into the tent.

"What is it, Father?"

"A stray dog from the last village attacked a lamb and tore a gash in its leg."

Leah grabbed the pouch of herbs in her part of the tent. Quickly she broke off a broad piece of fresh aloe. Taking the jar of yarrow salve, she dashed out of the tent.

Her father held the lamb. Kneeling on the ground, she cleansed the wound with the gelatinous inner portion of the aloe. The lamb cried and kicked while she worked on its leg. Soon the bleeding stopped. Then Leah applied yarrow salve to the wound.

"Let me hold it for a few minutes." She reached for the frightened lamb and gently tried to quiet its fears. The creature felt small and defenseless in her arms. The wool, soft and thick, was warm under her hands.

"Little lamb, little lamb," she sang, rocking back and forth on the ground. The lamb's struggles became weaker until at last it lay in her arms, blinking at the setting sun.

"You're a baby in my arms, aren't you?" She crooned to it. "Are you hungry, little one? I can't feed you. But I'll take you to your mother, and I'll pray to Jacob's God that He will keep you safe. Only one God. It's hard to believe. Maybe Jacob will tell me more about it."

She glanced up and saw Rachel walking toward the river with a water bag over her shoulder. Jacob strolled beside her. Leah watched them until the willows growing along the river hid them from view.

With a fierce longing, Leah hugged the lamb more tightly, and it struggled to escape her grasp. She let it limp away and she sat alone.

Zilpah came to stand beside her. "Are you all right, Mistress?"

Leah glanced up at her. "If only I had a chance, I could earn Jacob's love, couldn't I? Most men take more than one wife. If only he would ask for me, too, I know I could carry sons for him; then he would love me. If only I had a chance, I could earn his love."

The servant knelt down next to Leah. "A woman can't wait for a chance. She has to make opportunities."

"What do you mean?"

"Show him how capable you are at managing a household. Weave a new robe for him. Talk with him. Be tender and sympathetic."

"Do you think that would work well enough for him to ask for me, too?"

"You have seven years to make opportunities."

"Seven years," echoed Leah. "No! No! That's too long. Think how old I'll be. I can't wait that long."

She stared at the willows where the two had disappeared. The bushes parted. Jacob carried the heavy goatskin of water, Rachel walked beside him.

With new determination Leah repeated desperately, "Seven years. That's too long. I have to find a way to persuade Jacob to ask for me before he gets Rachel. He would never want me after he has her."

Chapter 5

Soon the sun vanished behind the western hills. Leah, Rachel, and the shepherd women has spaced the tents around the edges of a grassy meadow. Herded for the night into the center of the circle, the animals grazed in a more protected place rather than foraging up slopes and along the river.

Sheep-dung fires, sending up pale yellow flames, burned in front of each tent. Laban and Jacob sat cross-legged on reed mats near Leah's fire. She brought a clay pot of steaming boiled wheat flavored with thyme and onions and set it between the men, then returned with flat bread and goat cheese in a linen cloth.

The two men ripped off pieces of flat bread and used them to spoon the hot wheat into their mouths. The cheese they chewed along with the wheat.

"We made good distance today," Laban observed.

Jacob nodded. "All went well."

Leah retreated into the darkness beyond the light of the cooking fire. She watched the two men who were important in her life—Laban, her father, whom she admired and loved; Jacob, her kinsman, who was her hope for marriage, the man to fill her need for a husband.

"You have seven years to make opportunities," Zilpah had said. Long before the end of that time Leah hoped to convince him that he needed her for his wife. She must plan carefully and start right away, not letting any opportunity slip past. But what should she do? A complex plan began to formulate in her mind.

During the next two days the caravan journeyed farther north. Zilpah herded the milk goats ahead of her, and Leah drove the donkeys.

"I'm working on a plan so Jacob will want to ask for me in addition to Rachel," Leah confided to Zilpah. The maidservant nodded in approval. "Already I know he likes my cooking so I'll prepare his favorite foods as often as I can. I'll take a loom along when we go to winter pasture and weave him a robe."

"Good. You want him to become as dependent upon you as possible."

"I don't have the advantage that Rachel does. She's out in the pasture with him all day. My only chances are morning and evening and then there is so little time. Of course, I could walk out to the pasture . . ."

"Yes, you could go out to the pasture and speak with him."

"I will," Leah decided. Not only did she want to talk to him, but she had specific questions to ask. She wanted to know about his single God. She puzzled over what he had told her and Rachel about the Deity. If there was only one god, the Lord, did this mean that one god took care of everything? Did the Lord protect His people and also send angry storms? How could a male god help a woman in childbirth?

If she could find Jacob alone some time when her father and Rachel were not nearby, she could ask him about the Lord. Rachel objected when she talked alone with Jacob, and she knew her father would disapprove of any conversation about only one god.

Leah stared ahead to where her sister walked alongside the flocks. "I'll have to keep my plan secret," she told herself.

Two days later the caravan stopped in a wide valley dotted with small shrubs and isolated bunches of green grass. Here they would stay for a few weeks. The animals would forage all the new shoots of the scrubby bushes and graze on the supply of grass until only low stubble remained. Then Laban would move the flocks higher toward the northern mountain.

Once again the shepherd women pitched their tents in a wide circle around a flat pasture. The shepherds would take the flocks out to graze during the day and herd them back inside the circle at night, shunting the sheep to one side and the goats to the other. Divided, the animals remained more tranquil. Some shepherds watched over the animals during the night. They kept their slingshots and clubs ready to protect the flocks from roaming bears and wolves.

A stream ran through the valley. Years before, Laban's

shepherds had dug watering holes along the side of the stream and lined them with smooth stones. They diverted water from the rapidly flowing stream to form quiet pools with only a trickle of water. Here the sheep and goats drank without fear.

Now both men and women set about repairing the pools from winter damage. When they finished, the animals pushed forward to drink.

Leah and Zilpah gathered brush to start the cooking fire. "When will you go to visit Jacob in the pasture?" Zilpah asked.

"Tomorrow."

The following afternoon a cool breeze blew down from the mountains. Leah was glad for the spring sunshine that warmed her back. She rounded a hill to where Jacob watched the grazing sheep.

When he saw her, he called out in surprise, "What's happened? Is something wrong?" Hurrying to meet her, he stared toward the camp and held his slingshot in readiness.

The sight of his tall, strong figure rushing toward her set her heart to pounding. Did he care what happened to her? Or was he only concerned over the safety of the camp?

He stood near her. She glanced up into his deep-set brown eyes. Along with him, she was suddenly shy and let her gaze drop to the grass at her feet. "Nothing is wrong. I—I was just walking this way."

Her father would never approve of her searching for Jacob in the pasture, but now that she had dared to come, she would use the opportunity. She would ask the questions that filled her mind.

"You look like something is bothering you," he prompted gently.

Once again Leah looked up at him. She swallowed nervously. "I have a question. You said that there's only one god. How do you know that the Lord can protect my father's household and also protect your father's household when they are so far away?"

Jacob motioned to a flat outcropping of rock among the bunches of grass. "Sit down, Leah. I want to tell you how I know."

Resting on the stone, Leah pulled her robe over her goatskin boots and hugged her knees.

A light breeze ruffled his brown hair as he sat down on a stone opposite her. "My grandfather Abraham told my father and my father Isaac told me. One day the Lord appeared to my grandfather, and the Lord said He would give him all the land of Canaan and make a great nation of his descendants. The Lord established a covenant between Himself and my grandfather."

Jacob paused and stared down at the rocky soil. His voice took on a low, vibrant tone. "And then the Lord revealed that this covenant was between the two of them and all of my grandfather's descendants—from generation to generation—everlasting."

He raised his head and his eyes glowed with excitement. "Do you understand what that means? I already have a covenant with the Lord, and all of my descendants will have the covenant with the true God."

Leah sat in stunned silence. Would a god make a covenant with one man, a covenant that would pass to all the man's descendants? She had never thought of the possibility. It was too personal. Gods were distant beings represented by clay and bronze figures. They helped some of the time, but when they became angry, they could harm.

Jacob's tense enthusiasm held her spellbound. He seemed so sure. She began to catch something of his certainty.

The kinsman shifted on his rock. "Someday I'll return to the land of Canaan—the land that my sons will possess. You should see it—the rolling hills, the pastureland, the sea." He reached down among the grass at his feet and picked a small wild poppy that nestled there and handed the blossom to Leah. "The spring flowers are beautiful in Canaan."

The poppy lay like a tiny red cup in her hand. She looked from it into his face. With effort she drew her gaze back to the blossom. "Thank you," she murmured, realizing suddenly in her whole being that she wanted to say, "I love you, Jacob."

Quickly she rose to her feet and headed back toward the camp, cradling the flower between her hands.

A voice startled her—Rachel's! Her sister stood up from behind a boulder. "What did Jacob give you?"

Leah opened her hands and showed the delicate flower. "A poppy."

Rachel's eyes blazed with anger. "You shouldn't accept anything from him. I'm betrothed to him. You are not. Leave him alone. He's mine."

"I was just asking him—he was telling me—he was telling me about the land of Canaan."

"Give me that flower." Rachel grabbed for it.

Leah jumped away. "No. It's mine. He gave it to me." She ran across the meadow toward the camp. Inside the tent she placed the poppy in an embroidered head scarf and hid it in the bottom of her clothes basket.

Whenever Rachel or her father was out of sight, Leah talked with Jacob. He spoke freely about his God, and she listened attentively. She was uncomfortably aware that he objected to the household gods in the tent. Eventually she stopped asking them for protection. One day she glanced at them and a shudder ran through her. Quickly she closed her eyes and whispered, "Lord, God of Jacob, protect me."

A few weeks later Laban moved his flocks to higher pasture. One night as Leah lay next to her sister on their sheepskins, Rachel confided to her, "Jacob told me more about his Lord."

"Yes, he told me, too," Leah answered, "and I think I've come to trust the Lord like he does."

"I think I also trust the Lord, but I like the other gods, too, especially the goddess of love and her baby. I can't give her up."

"Jacob is sure he knows best. You should try to stop worshiping her."

"I can't. I can't."

Early one morning four months later Leah lifted the tent flap and blinked against the brightness of sunshine on frosty ground. She looked up at the northern mountains. A sprinkling of fresh snow covered their jagged tops.

Laban came out of his tent and gazed up at the mountains. Snow—the signal for him to lead his flocks and his people southward to Haran. There they would stay for about a month before leaving for winter in the south. The pastureland around Haran couldn't support his animals for more than a month this time of the year.

"I've been expecting this snow the last few days," he said to Leah. "Start packing. We'll head toward Haran today."

Jacob arrived from the meadow and sat down, huddled in his square-cut sheepskin cloak. The wool was turned to the inside to protect him against cold nights in the field.

Leah hastened to build the fire. From a leather saddlebag she took her fire-lighting tools—pyrite and flint. She reached into the bag again and brought out tinder—dry grass and thistle down. Using hard, sure strokes she struck the gray flint against the golden pyrite. Sparks flew onto the tinder, causing it to smolder.

Quickly she placed dry twigs onto the smoking tinder and blew on them until they burst into flame. From a basket she added dried sheep dung.

Yawning, Rachel came out of the tent. "My turn to watch the sheep." She smiled at Jacob, and as she strolled past him she ran her hand lightly across his broad shoulders.

He swung around to watch her walk toward the pasture. Then returning to the fire, he spread out his hands to warm them over the blaze. A wide smile spread across his face. "She's beautiful. Beautiful."

Her mouth a thin line, Leah threw more dung on the fire and went into the tent to pack.

The caravan traveled slowly down from the northern mountains, staying a few days at various camps. After three weeks they arrived at home pastureland. Leah and Zilpah drove the donkeys to the house in Haran.

Two days later Laban summoned his daughters into his room. "Today I'm going to the matchmaker to arrange for a wife for myself," he announced bluntly. "I've already put it off too long. I must have sons."

Extending his arms, he drew the two of them to him, one on each side the way he had held them when they were children. He leaned his head down to receive their kisses on his cheeks.

"Yes, Father."

"Of course, Father."

Although their words affirmed his decision, he heard hesitancy in their voices.

They watched his tall figure go out the door and through the courtyard gate. Rachel turned to Leah. The sisters hugged each other, their jealousy over Jacob forgotten for the moment. Awareness of a new threat surrounded them.

"I can hardly remember our mother," Rachel said apprehensively. "You're the only mother I've known. What will it be like when Father brings another woman into the house?"

"I don't know," Leah responded with equal concern. "I just don't know."

As Laban headed toward the marketplace, he tried to sort out his thoughts. Why had he waited all these years before

45

taking a new wife? How long had it been? Nine years—nine years since his wife died while giving birth to his stillborn son. Fear that he might never plant seed for sons lurked in the deeper recesses of his mind. He recoiled against the thought of failure.

Yet a man must have sons. The only recourse was to find an appropriate woman. He didn't consider himself an old man, but still the years were passing—and he needed sons.

Near the marketplace he turned into a crooked passageway that wound between windowless walls. At a small wooden door he knocked loudly.

A servant's voice shouted through the barrier, "Who?"

"Laban, the sheepman."

The door opened inward, and Laban stepped across a stone threshold into a small courtyard. An apricot tree grew in the center, and under it woven reed mats formed a sitting place.

The matchmaker came out of his dome-shaped mud-brick house. A short, fat man with small, soft hands, he was a complete contrast to Laban's tall, muscled figure and hard, work-worn hands.

The matchmaker bowed respectfully to his guest. "Welcome, Laban, owner of sheep and goats. Enter my humble home." Inside the room the matchmaker motioned to a woolen rug, brightly woven in red and white stripes. "Seat yourself."

Laban took a cross-legged position. The matchmaker snapped his fingers at a slave woman, indicating she should bring wine for the guest.

With the goblet of wine in front of him, Laban waited for the proper formalities.

The matchmaker seated himself on a brown-and-white rug opposite his guest. "How is your family?"

"All are well."

"I hear you have a kinsman, a nephew living with you."

"He is well."

"How is your business?"

For once Laban became impatient with formalities. He fidgeted with his mustache and ran his hand over his beard. "My business is fine, but I'm here for another purpose."

The matchmaker nodded his head. "What can I do for you?"

"I need a wife, but I don't want a young girl of the usual marrying age. I want an older one."

The matchmaker rubbed his plump hand across his forehead. "Let me think. I have a limited number right now but, yes,

46

here is a possibility. The daughter of Enthur the spice merchant. Let me explain. She developed a little late. At last she was promised, but before the betrothal with witnesses the young man became drunk and fell off his camel. He will recover, but the spice merchant Enthur refuses to accept him for his daughter."

The matchmaker reached into a cedar chest and drew out a clay tablet. "See. Here is the contract that I prepared. I expected Enthur to sign before the clay dried, but, as you can see, the place for his signature and the signatures of the two witnesses is blank."

"How old is this daughter of Enthur?"

"Well into marrying age. She is 15 already, and no man has known her. Since she is of this age, the bride-price would be less than usual."

Laban frowned. Fifteen! He didn't need another young girl in the house. Already he lacked peace and quiet with Rachel and Leah and the two chattering maidservants. And then there was the matter of a woman's ability to successfully carry his seed.

"I'm past the age when I need a girl who has never known a man. I need a woman who has proved she can carry a man's son until the child is ready to see the light of day."

The matchmaker nodded in understanding. "Enthur the spice merchant has three daughters. There is an older one. Her husband died and left her with four sons. She lives now with the sons in her father's house. The bride-price would cost little, but there is the matter of the four sons. They belong to Enthur, of course, so if you want the sons, the price would run higher."

"I do not care to bring up another man's sons," Laban replied decisively. "I plan to raise my own."

"Very well. Do you wish to have me contact Enthur and arrange for you to take a look at the woman?"

"You may contact Enthur. Tell him that if I like the appearance of his daughter and if the bride price is satisfactory, I would be interested. Since the woman is a widow, I expect him to waive the usual year's betrothal time. I will sign the contract, but I expect to claim the woman after spring sheepshearing."

The men rose to their feet, and the matchmaker bowed. "As you know, my fee is set by law, but at any time I might consider accepting the gift of a lamb prepared for roasting."

"If and when I sign the contract, you shall have your fee and a lamb."

As Laban returned slowly down the narrow street, his thoughts shifted from Enthur's daughter with the four sons to his own wife who had died nine years before. Although she carried only his two daughters successfully, although she failed him by dying instead of giving him the son he had planted in her, he remembered her fondly. She had managed the household efficiently. She was tender and kind. She loved him.

He paused and lifted his hand to his beard. The realization came like a rush of wind. He had loved her too.

The following week Laban signed the contract with Enthur for the spice merchant's widowed daughter. He paid the matchmaker his fee and sent Gamesh with the lamb. Then he hired bricklayers to build a new room on his house. It would encroach on courtyard space, but was necessary for the new wife and his future sons.

Before the month passed, Leah began to gather provisions and equipment for the trek to winter pasture. She made a quick trip to the wool merchant for brown, red, black, and white woolen yarn. A portable loom fit onto a donkey over baskets of wheat and barley. Leah would weave a new robe for Jacob during winter pasture.

In winter camp cold winds roared down from the northwest. Leah hung woven woolen coverings over the openings of the tent's center space. Smoke from a fire on a hearth of stones swirled up and out a hole in the ceiling. With the loom placed near the warmth of the fire, she worked long hours producing fabric for Jacob's new robe. Zilpah stitched it together.

One cold evening Leah presented the finished robe to Jacob. He ran his hands over the brown, red, black, and white stripes. His smile was her thanks.

She bowed her head and clasped her hands behind her. "I'm glad you like it," she murmured.

Winter passed. Laban led his flocks back to Haran. After lambing and shearing he provided the usual feast. The next evening he went to Enthur the spice merchant's house to claim his new wife and brought her home without the elaborate festivities of a first marriage.

Leah and Rachel peeked out the door of their room at the heavily veiled woman. Flickering torches in the courtyard revealed only her long robe and the thick veil that covered her from head to feet. She followed their father into the newly completed room of the house.

"I wonder what she looks like," Rachel whispered.

"We'll find out in the morning," Leah answered in a hushed voice.

The following morning, long after Laban and Rachel had gone out to the pasture, the woman finally left her room. She slowly crossed the courtyard to stand squarely on the other side of the worktable from Leah. Shorter than Leah, she had pulled her dark hair back from her plump face into an untidy tail tied crudely with a woven ribbon. Her gray eyes carried no warmth.

"I am Ahera, your father's wife," she announced.

Flattening out a piece of bread dough, Leah answered, "I am Leah, the firstborn of my father."

Ahera reached into the bowl for a handful of dough. "I will bake the bread for my husband." Dry flour spilled onto the brick floor.

Leah stepped away from the table. "Bilhah, bring a broom to sweep up this flour."

"Yes, Mistress Leah."

"I will decide when to clean up spilled flour," Ahera warned. "I am the mistress of this household. And you will call me 'Mother Ahera' with the respect due to your father's wife."

"Yes—yes—Moth—Mother Ahera." Slowly Leah placed the flattened dough onto a hot stone. "And I will bake the bread for Jacob."

Preparations for summer pasture progressed chaotically. Ahera insisted on overseeing the packing, but as a spice merchant's daughter, she had no experience in the needs for nomadic life.

Leah knew that the tent must have an additional room. With no time to weave the necessary strips, she would have to remove some from her own tent and take others from Rachel's unfinished one.

In frustration she went to the lean-to shed in the donkey enclosure where she stored her tent. Her hands lovingly caressed the coarse black, brown, and red goat hair. Would she ever need her tent? Would she ever have a husband?

Straightening, she called Zilpah to rip some strips off it and sew them onto her father's.

A year passed in disordered confusion. Ahera gave birth to a son, but the household suffered from lack of attention.

When the baby was 2 months old, Leah's frustrations surfaced. The new wife had allowed the supply of wheat and barley to become low.

Leaving the storeroom, Leah reluctantly went to the courtyard where her stepmother sat on a low stool. "Shall I go to the market for grain?"

"I will send Gamesh," the woman answered.

"But that slave boy doesn't know how to bargain."

"I will decide who goes to market." Ahera returned to her room to nurse her infant.

Leah stared after her, and then with tears of anger in her eyes she stumbled to the back wall where her herb garden flourished. There she squatted down by a large-leafed comfrey plant. Even in the heat of her resentment, she noticed and admired the lavender, bell-shaped blossoms on the plant. Next to it sturdy thyme sent out a pungent aroma from its small leaves and tiny pale orchid flowers. Coriander spread lacy white blossoms on top of tell slender stalks.

In the comfort of her garden Leah's thoughts turned to Jacob. She pondered over her plan to earn his approval. He accepted her cooking. He appeared pleased with his robe. Yet, as far as she knew, he was no nearer to asking for her than he had been two years ago.

As she knelt by a mint plant, a wave of despair swept over her. She needed someone to love her. Jacob—she needed him. Time was passing too quickly. Most women her age had four or five children already. She was 19 years old. Too old. Too old. Her desire, though, was more than just for a husband, a man to father children. She wanted Jacob. An intense yearning for him enveloped her. She desired no other man. Jacob was the man she loved.

The mint plant in front of her swayed in the breeze. Picking a leaf, she rubbed it between her fingers, inhaling the scent. How could she make him want her? The aroma from the mint leaf faded. He wanted Rachel. Jacob was always happy when her sister was near him. He didn't need anyone else. A tear fell on the mint plant. So far her plan was not working.

Leah picked another mint leaf and inhaled. She would not give up her quest for Jacob's love.

While she knelt in her herb garden, her father stood in the

pasture and surveyed his flocks. Each spring after shearing season he reviewed the progress of the year. Now he nodded his head in satisfaction. With Jacob's good management the flocks had increased more than usual during the past year. Laban had sold a record amount of wool and goat hair.

He thought of the year's events at his house. Ahera had successfully carried a son. He hoped she would do the same each year.

His hope was fulfilled. The following spring he had another son. Then came a delay of a few months, but by the end of summer pasture another had arrived. Ahera managed the house poorly, but she incubated his seed well.

As for the sheep and goats, the flocks continued to increase. Jacob knew the business better than any shepherd Laban had ever hired. He and his nephew worked well together, and he was satisfied with the younger man's abilities.

One shearing season Laban counted the years and realized with a start that six years had passed since he and Jacob had agreed on a bride price. In another year his nephew would pay off the dowry for Rachel. Then he would surely want to return to his homeland. Laban turned the possibility around in his mind.

But why not keep Jacob in Haran awhile longer? Why not?

Chapter 6

Thorn bushes infested the south where Laban pastured his flocks the following winter. One day Jacob came to Leah and held out his hand. "Do you have an herb to help this?" Dried blood covered deep scratches.

"What happened?"

"A ram caught its horns in a bush. While I was wrestling it out of the branches, I got my hand into the thorns."

"I'll get aloe." She rushed into the tent for her supplies and came out with a jug of water, a wad of wool, and a piece of aloe.

Jacob sat down on a stone, and Leah knelt beside him. "First let me cleanse the wound." Holding his arm gently with one hand, she used the water-soaked wool to sponge away the dried blood. Taking the aloe, she pulled back the outer layer of the leaf and applied the soothing inner gel, spreading it thickly over all the scratches.

Her fingers tingled as she touched his strong arm and hand. She let her hands linger. "Please hold still until the aloe gel dries."

Jacob sat contentedly in front of her with his arm resting on her hands. "You know a good deal about curing wounds and illnesses, don't you?"

"My mother taught me. She taught me to weave, too, and to care for the household. I was 8 years old when she died, old enough to take some responsibility."

"Has it been hard for you since your father brought home a new wife?"

Leah dared not look at him. The thought was painful. Ahera had taken over as mistress of the household and tried to shut her off from her father. Ahera's messy housekeeping still frustrated her to the point that she might cry if she spoke of it. All she could answer was "It's hard."

She looked up in time to catch an expression of sympathy flicker across his face. Then he said, "My hand feels better now. I'll be getting back to the pasture."

As she watched him walk away, she clasped her hands together, the hands that had so recently held his hand and arm in hers. Raising them to her lips she kissed the fingers that had touched him.

Rachel's voice whipped across her. "I saw you. I saw you holding Jacob's hand."

Leah jerked her fingers away from her mouth. "I was applying aloe to his scratches."

"You didn't have to hold his arm so long."

"The gel has to dry."

"Ha! You know it didn't need to dry that long. That was an excuse to touch him. You leave him alone. He's mine. Why didn't you send him to me so I could take care of his scratches?"

"He came to me. When he asked for help, I gave it to him."

The girl's head drooped. "Why didn't he come to me?" she asked faintly.

"Rachel, everyone knows he loves you. Please don't be jealous because he asked me to help him."

"I'm more than jealous." Her voice grew stronger. "I'm restless and edgy and uneasy. Oh, Leah, it's so hard to wait. Father shouldn't have made Jacob and me wait seven years. That's too long. Besides wanting him so much, all this time I've been afraid Jacob would get tired of waiting. I thought he might go back to Canaan before the time was up."

"He wouldn't do that," Leah exclaimed in disbelief.

Her sister sighed heavily. "I was afraid, but now when shearing time is over, I'll have him at last."

Leah turned away to hide her own frustration.

They came up to Haran from winter pasture. Some of the ewes gave birth to their lambs, and shearing started.

Jacob walked over from the shearing ground and dropped wool on the pile at Laban's feet. He wiped sweat from his forehead with the back of his hand. "Good, hard work, this shearing," he said.

"It's hard work, all right, and for good rewards. This wool will bring an excellent price."

The younger man glanced toward the flock where Rachel kept the milling sheep and goats from straying too far from the shearers. His gaze rested on her and he smiled. "I'm ready for my reward."

Laban stooped down to finger the wool. "What reward do you have in mind?"

His nephew stood above him. "My wages, of course. I've completed my time and my part of the agreement. I want my wife. I've worked seven years in exchange for her."

Jacob glanced toward his betrothed once more, Laban, the faintest hint of a smile lurking around his lips, following his gaze. Rachel had always been happy among the animals. She moved lightheartedly like one of the young lambs. Now it struck him suddenly that during these seven years his slim little daughter had rounded out into a beautiful woman.

"I've worked for seven years," Jacob repeated. "That was our agreement."

"You shall have your wife."

"When shall I have her?"

"As soon as we complete the shearing, I'll invite my friends and make the wedding feasts."

Leaving Laban by the pile of wool, Jacob returned to the flock. Laban saw him stop to say something to Rachel. They made a handsome couple—he with strong shoulders from working among the sheep. It took strength and muscle to hold the animals securely for shearing. Rachel drifted through the flock like a living goddess—a little too slender perhaps, but evidently attractive to Jacob.

How easy it had been to find a man who wanted to marry her—not so easy to find one for Leah. Why couldn't men see the advantages of the older daughter? She was the same height as Rachel but better developed—able to bear a young man's many sons.

The years were passing and she was long past marrying age. How old was she now? Twenty-four, perhaps? He shook his head and shifted his attention from Jacob and Rachel to the scene before him—shepherds shearing sheep and goats. The earthy smell of wool usually gave him a secure feeling. Ordinarily he liked this time of the year—woolen fleeces piling up, merchants coming to buy, gold and silver adding up in his pouch.

This spring, however, he felt an apprehension.

Business had prospered under Jacob's guidance. He had proved himself a valuable asset, but Laban suspected that his kinsman was staying only until he married Rachel. Then he planned to take his wife back to Canaan.

"Not if I can prevent it," Laban muttered.

He smiled in satisfaction as he remembered the good bride price he had extracted. Laban felt pleased with himself. He had bargained well when he promised Rachel in marriage. Jacob had paid with seven years of labor, and during those years Laban had taken time to plan for the future.

He glanced again toward the flocks. His nephew still talked with his younger daughter. Laban turned away from the shearing ground and strode across the fields toward his house.

The walk across the fields felt good. The spring air braced his spirits.

Two problems challenged him—how to keep his most efficient and hardworking shepherd, and how to arrange a marriage for Leah. He enjoyed challenges when he had solutions in mind. Now he felt confident he could solve his two problems quite simply with one answer.

In his mind he pictured a wedding feast—the men eating and drinking while the bride waited in her room. Now if the groom had sufficient wine and the bride's veil was heavy enough, and since it was the custom for the bride to remain silent on her wedding day, and since Leah and Rachel were the same height . . . Of course, he was willing to give Rachel later—for a good bride-price.

In the courtyard Leah sat on a stool, spring sunshine warming her back. She faced the extra room her father had built on the house six years ago before he married the young widow. Now two sturdy boys played by the door to the room. They were Kesad and Jabal, Leah's half-brothers. Even though her stepmother was a slovenly housekeeper, Leah knew her father was pleased that Ahera was filling the house with sons for him. Right now she was in the room nursing her newest male child.

While Leah rested, her hands were still busy. Occasionally, instead of buying from the wool merchant, she enjoyed spinning her own yarn. The routine had a calming effect. Using a spindle, she twisted clean, carded wool into knobby yarn. The wool slid steadily through her fingers, leaving them soft and smooth from the oil. She paused to wind the yarn into a thick ball and then carried it to the loom to continue her weaving.

Ahera emerged from her room, holding her baby on her plump hip. Leah had never adjusted to calling her "Mother Ahera," but she did when necessary. Glancing up from her weaving, she smiled at the baby.

Ahera stood next to the loom. "Your father needs to add another room onto this house," she stated flatly.

"Another room onto the house?" She knew why, but her mind resisted acceptance of the reason.

"Of course. After Jacob and Rachel are married, she will need a room of her own. She can't share yours. You know that."

"Of course Rachel will need a room," Leah echoed.

"You'll have to ask your father to build the room," Ahera insisted. "When it comes to household business, he never listens to me or to Rachel. You're the only one who can talk to him about building the room. So you'll have to ask him."

"I suppose I'll have to ask him to build it." Leah resigned herself to the assignment. "I'll talk to him as soon as possible."

Ahera carried the baby into her room, and Leah turned her attention back to her work. The pattern in the weaving blurred before her eyes. How much nicer it would feel if the room were for herself instead of for Rachel.

"Leah!" Her father strode into the courtyard. It surprised her that he had come home so early from the shearing.

She got up from the loom and went to him. "What's wrong, Father?"

"Nothing's wrong. Come with me. I want to talk to you."

She followed him into his room—Jacob's room, too. As usual she was aware of her father's household gods arrayed along the brick shelf that jutted from the wall. Folded sheepskins rested in a corner. Jacob's robe was thrown over a large basket.

"What is it you want, Father?"

"Sit down. I have something important to tell you."

Leah positioned herself on a cushion. Clearing his throat, her father announced, "You're going to be married."

She detected the authority in his voice, and her heart skipped.

"Married? Who—who will marry me?" Somehow she had a hard time making any words come out.

"It's not important who is going to marry you. Aren't you going to thank your father for arranging your marriage?"

"Yes, of course, Father. I'm very grateful. Thank you. Thank you, but who—?"

"All right. It's Jacob."

"Jacob! But Rachel—"

"Never mind Rachel." His irritated words stabbed into her mind. "You're older. You must marry first."

"I know I'm supposed to marry first, but what does Jacob say about this?" she asked in a barely audible voice.

"He doesn't know, and you won't tell him."

Then the realization of her father's scheme hit her. She knew about substitutions on wedding nights, and it had occurred to her that her father might plan such a thing for her. Deep inside she knew that he never intended for Rachel to marry first. She had wondered how he would plan to save her from shame.

"Father, how will you arrange my marriage?" she asked steadily.

"Now listen carefully so you'll know what you are supposed to do." Her father also spoke matter-of-factly. "After the feast on the first night of the wedding week, I'll take Jacob to the bridal chamber. Of course you'll be wearing the traditional veil, so he won't see you; and you'll remain silent as is proper for the bride, so he won't hear your voice."

Leah stood up and faced her father. "Jacob will be furious when he finds out. He doesn't want to marry me. He loves Rachel."

"Marriage isn't for love," Laban roared. "A man takes a wife to carry his seed and produce sons for him."

"I'm sure I can earn his love with sons, but in the meantime he'll hate me." Tears filled her eyes.

"Now don't start weeping. Are you objecting to something I'm doing for your own good? Stop crying. This is the way it's going to be." Leah had never heard his voice so inflexible, even when he bargained over the price of his wool.

"I'm not objecting, Father," she answered. "I just don't like the thought of him hating me."

"He won't hate you if you give him his sons. You're a woman, aren't you? It's your duty to produce sons."

"And I'm wondering if it's right to deceive a kinsman."

"For a woman you think too much. Leave all this in my hands. I know what I'm doing." Laban stalked out of the room.

Leah sank down onto the cushion again.

Jacob's wife! The one place she longed most to be was in his arms. She had long daydreamed of how she might become his wife. For years she had pictured him saying to her father, "I've learned to love Leah and I want her for my wife." Of course that hadn't happened.

"Are you objecting?" her father had asked.

Was she? No, no, never!

But I'm afraid, she thought as she closed her eyes and began to sway silently back and forth. *I want Jacob's love. Could he learn to love me if I give him sons? How wonderful it would be to hold my own babies in my arms, to nurse them at my breast, to love them, to watch them grow into men who would look like Jacob.*

Her father was right. The older daughter must marry first. Never had she disobeyed him. She mustn't rebel against his authority nor against tradition, even if it meant she had to become part of a deceitful scheme against the man she loved.

When she opened her eyes, the household gods gazed at her with blank expressions. They offered no help. She shivered. Quickly she ran out of the room into the courtyard where the sun warmed her upturned face.

"Lord, help me. I'm afraid, so afraid."

Chapter 7

Zilpah," Leah whispered, breaking the silence she was supposed to maintain on her wedding day. "I'm afraid."

"Yes, I know," the servant answered also in a whisper. "I'd be afraid too if this were happening to me." She helped Leah into the wedding robe, richly embroidered with bright blue and red silk thread. The fringe of the garment brushed her ankles. Draped over a basket, a head-to-foot veil lay ready.

Leah's voice trembled. "Jacob will hate me for deceiving him."

"Mistress, it's really Master Laban who is doing the deceiving."

"I'm guilty too. I agreed to my father's plan, and don't forget I'm the one who will be here when Jacob finds out."

Zilpah picked up an ivory comb and started to smooth the bride-to-be's long, brown hair. "Where's Rachel?" Leah asked.

"In your stepmother's room. Mistress Ahera is keeping her out of sight."

"I'm glad I'm not Rachel today," Leah said softly.

Midmorning sunlight sifted in through the window slits. Sounds of preparation for the wedding feast came from the courtyard. Laban had hired extra cooks to roast lambs, bake bread, and prepare large pots of boiled wheat. He had ordered baskets of cucumbers and onions, and he had gone to the wine merchants for the choicest wines. Raisins, dates, and fig cakes lay ready on trays.

The savory smell from roasting lambs drifted into the room where Zilpah combed Leah's hair.

A burst of laughter sounded from the courtyard. The servant woman peeked out the door. "The wedding guests are coming.

59

I see shepherds and some merchants. There's the wool merchant Teshar."

"Close the door," Leah whispered urgently. "If Teshar had asked for me instead of Rachel, all this wouldn't be happening."

"Would you rather have Master Teshar instead of Master Jacob?"

"Of course not. It's just that I'm so frightened. If I were marrying Teshar, he would know ahead of time."

A few minutes later Laban opened the door to Leah's room. "Zilpah," he inquired, "is the bridal chamber in order?"

"Yes, Master Laban." She pointed to the floor. "I have laid out the sheepskins. I've sprinkled the linen bridal sheet with cinnamon for fragrance and I've brought in oleander blossoms for a sweet smell."

"You haven't put the jewelry on the bride's head yet." Impatience edged his voice. "Women are waiting outside the gate to pay their respects to the bride."

"I'll arrange the necklaces and bracelets right away," the handmaiden promised.

"Don't forget the perfume. I paid an unreasonable price for it."

"No, Master Laban, I won't forget the perfume."

"Daughter," he addressed Leah, "I have a gift for you." She looked at her father, but dutifully remained silent. "I'm giving you Zilpah."

Leah stood on her tiptoes to kiss her father's cheek. It was a generous gift and one she appreciated. He knew how much she depended upon the woman.

Laban kissed Leah and then returned to Jacob and his guests.

"I'm happy Master Laban gave me to you," Zilpah whispered

"So am I," her mistress answered. "Do you remember the day my father brought you and Bilhah home from the slave market? I was only 7 years old, and you were even younger."

Zilpah nodded her head. "Your mother asked your father, 'Why have you bought these two skinny little girls?' and he said, 'I got them at a good price off a caravan from Egypt.' "

"Mother wanted a slave woman to help with the cooking and to wait on my grandmother because her eyesight was too poor for her to take care of herself, but Father thought two girls were a better use for his money."

Another burst of laughter filled the courtyard. Hired entertainers struck the first notes on their musical instruments. The twang from harp strings and the drumbeat from tabrets vibrated through the morning air.

"I wish I could stop shaking," Leah said.

"Please sit down, Mistress, so I can put the jewelry on you. You'll feel better then, but first I'll rub on the perfume."

Zilpah removed the lid from a small ivory jar. A heavy scent rose from the perfume—musk imported from a more eastern land. She smoothed the mixture of musk powder and sesame oil across Leah's forehead, working it into her temples, applying it liberally to ears, neck, wrists, and ankles. The strong scent filled the room.

Next Zilpah slipped gold and silver bracelets onto Leah's wrists. She draped a string of gold disks around her neck. Then, after the handmaiden arranged the long veil over her head, Leah stood up. The veil covered her completely, reaching all the way to the floor, hiding her bare feet. Zilpah placed another set of gold disks over Leah's forehead and a garland of oleander blossoms around her head on top of the veil.

Now dressed and adorned, Leah sat down on a low stool and waited for her guests. Zilpah opened the door and motioned for another servant to let the women in the gate. They crowded into the room—wives and daughters of the merchants and shepherds, Teshar's mother and four sister. Carefully avoiding the bridal bed of sheepskins, they surrounded the bride, commenting on the embroidery of her veil, the shine of her jewelry, the aroma of her perfume.

Her head bowed, Leah maintained complete silence. *Will one of these women recognize me?* she wondered. Her hands felt wet and she shivered although the room had seemed too warm moments before.

Bilhah came in with a large tray of wheat bread and fig cakes. The women nibbled the refreshments and continued to exclaim about the bride. Finally they sat on the rugs that covered the floor. They told stories of their wedding celebrations and the birth of their children.

More women came until the room was packed with as many as it could hold. Bilhah brought dates, raisins, and more bread. Hours passed.

From the courtyard loud male voices and laughter indicated that Laban's guests were appreciating the food and drink. The musicians' voices rose in the wedding songs.

Throughout the day Leah's thoughts returned often to Rachel and to information her sister had given her early that morning. It brought a dread that she refused to share even with Zilpah.

"Jacob suspects something," Rachel had told her. "He knows that Father believes strongly in tradition and he suspects that Father might substitute you for me tonight. So Jacob and I have agreed on a secret signal."

It stunned Leah. "So even though I'm covered with the long veil, Father's plan won't work."

"Father's plan will work."

"How can it? I won't know the signal, and Jacob will find out right away it isn't you."

"It will work because I'm going to tell you the secret signal."

Leah gasped in surprise. "Why—why would you want to tell me your secret?"

"Father says he'll let Jacob marry me too. But I'm afraid." Her voice shook. "Jacob wants to go back to Canaan. I'm afraid if he finds out that Father is substituting you tonight, he might become angry enough to leave without marrying either one of us."

"Do you really think he would?" Leah clutched her hands together. "Do you think he would leave for Canaan without marrying either of us? No, No! We can't let him do that."

"Then I'll tell you the secret." Rachel wiped away a tear with the back of her hand and took a deep breath. Her body stiff, her eyes closed, she revealed the signal in a flat, fiercely controlled voice.

Now hours later Leah sat on the stool. She trembled when she thought of Jacob coming to her. At last Zilpah lit oil lamps in the room, then peeked out the door. "The sun has gone down. One of the hired servants is lighting torches."

As the night grew darker, some of the women left the room and stood in the shadow of the courtyard wall. They watched the men at the feast tables and waited for the final moments of the marriage celebration. The men renewed their shouting and laughter, the musicians intensified the beat of the tabrets.

"Here comes the bridegroom," the men hollered to let the bride know. "Here he is!" The drums beat a fast rhythm and timbrels jangled.

Laban opened the door. The bride's guests filed out. Zilpah

touched Leah's arm and then followed the women.

Leah stood alone in the dimly lit room. Heavy fragrance enveloped her—musk perfume mixed with the scent of burning olive oil in the lamps. She tried to take a deep breath but found it impossible.

Her father stepped in and took her hand, his fingers warm against her cold ones. Clinging to him, not wanting to let go, she pulled back toward the wall.

"Come, daughter." Her father's strong voice stopped her retreat. "We're ready for the next part of the wedding celebration. I'm going to present you to the groom."

He led her toward the door. Through her veil she could make out a dark form silhouetted against the torchlight. Jacob! "Here is your bride. Go in to her," she heard her father say. He placed her hand into Jacob's. She sensed a tingle of excitement from his tight grasp. He entered the room. Could he see through her veil? How soon would he discover she was Leah, not Rachel? Again she trembled. Her father blew out the oil lamps.

"My blessings on this marriage," he said. Then he vanished into the courtyard.

The formal wedding ceremony was complete.

Leah felt the strength of Jacob's hand as he led her away from the closed door. In the darkness of the room she heard his breathing. She smelled the frankincense and myrrh that the men had rubbed onto his forehead. His fingers slid up her arm to the back of her neck. She tried to hold back the sound of her weeping.

"Don't cry," he reassured her. "I'll treat you gently."

He reached for her veil and pulled it off her head, tumbling the garland of oleander blossoms and the gold disks to the rugs on the floor. Next he took off the jewelry from around her neck. She shivered from the touch of his hands.

Then he held her close and waited. The secret signal—now was the time when she must give him the signal.

She slipped from his arms and sank slowly to her knees. Taking his left hand in both of hers, turning the palm up, she kissed it lightly. Then she took his right hand and kissed the palm. Standing on tiptoe, she pulled his head down so she could kiss his forehead. At last her lips rested on his. His breath smelled of wine and fig cakes.

He gave a happy laugh.

She and her father had successfully deceived him. After he

found out, would he ever come to her again? At least she could hold him close for this one night.

Later she lay awake for a long time, listening to his measured breaths as he slept next to her. Far into the night she heard muffled weeping—Rachel, probably huddled in a corner of their stepmother's room. Rachel, sobbing out the disappointment of her lost wedding night.

Jacob moved in his sleep and reached for her. Leah held completely still, not daring even to breathe for a moment.

Cold fear came again. How angry he would be when he saw her in the morning. What would he do?

Chapter 8

Faint light filtering through the window slit woke her. Her first awareness was of his broad back—warm against hers. She lay still, afraid to move, dreading his anger, overcome with fear that he would hate her for deceiving him.

The light through the window slit gave only shadowy shapes to the familiar objects in this room that she usually shared with Rachel—bolsters and cushions piled against a wall—two wicker baskets, one for her clothes, one for Rachel's. Her father had agreed to build a new room for Rachel, but it was only half finished. The bricklayers still worked on it.

Jacob stirred and turned over to face her. Leah held her breath. He reached for her as he had during the night, his beard brushing her cheek while his hand caressed her back. She wanted to lie in his arms, but her fear caused her body to tense.

He opened his eyes. For an unbelievably long moment he stared at her. She felt the muscles in his arms constrict.

"You!" he gasped hoarsely. "What are you doing here? Where's Rachel?" Abruptly he sat up. Leah cowered under the woolen robe that had covered them through the night. Trying to hide from his anger, she squeezed her eyes shut.

Jacob grabbed her and jerked her to a sitting position. The robe fell away from her bare shoulders. Shaking her, he demanded, "Answer me. What are you doing here? Where's Rachel?"

"I'm older. Father said—"

"What have you done to me? Your whole family has deceived me. Leah, I trusted you. I never thought you would deceive me. And Rachel. I trusted her, too." He covered his eyes with his hand. "Last night you gave me the secret signal. Rachel told you, didn't she? Why would she do this to me?"

"She said—"

"I don't want to hear what she said. Get away from me." Jacob shoved her away from him, and she fell backward onto a rug. "You and your father have tricked me. I should have known I couldn't trust Laban to keep his agreement."

Leaping up from the sheepskin bed, he reached for his tunic and robe. "I'm going to find your father and have this out with him. I worked seven years for Rachel. I didn't mind—she's worth it. I'll have her yet. Your father isn't going to get away with this scheme."

Laban had slept poorly. Through the wall to his wife's room he heard Rachel crying in the night. He got up early and paced restlessly in his room. Now he heard Jacob's footsteps in the courtyard.

As he stepped into the courtyard to face his son-in-law, the first ray of sunlight touched the top of the wall. His trained ear heard the bleating of sheep in the distance. Putting his hand on his beard, he braced himself for the confrontation. "Good morning," he said. "I didn't expect you out of the bridal chamber this time of day."

"Why have you done this to me?" Jacob thrust himself in front of the older man. "Seven years, Laban. Didn't I serve you seven years for Rachel? Why have you deceived me? Why have you given me Leah instead of Rachel?"

"I promised you one of my daughters for your wife. You have her."

"We agreed on Rachel. You know you promised Rachel."

In her room Leah heard the loud, angry voices of her father and her husband. Hastily she pulled on her white woolen robe, then, covering her face with her hands, sank down on the sheepskins.

Her father's words came clearly from the courtyard. "Are you unhappy because you think my daughter Leah was not a virgin? We'll see about that."

"That has nothing to do with it," Jacob shouted. "I worked for Rachel. Why have you substituted Leah? Just because you could not find a husband for her, you have no right to force her on me! Couldn't you get rid of her any other way?"

"Your words are unkind, Jacob." Laban lowered his voice. "They are also unnecessary. You know I follow the traditions of my people. It is our custom to give the older before the younger.

You've lived here long enough to know that."

The son-in-law glared at him. "You mean it's the custom, even with a witnessed agreement that says you promised the younger?"

Laban shrugged. "Where are these witnesses now? One was my old friend who has died. The other leads a caravan. Only the gods know where he travels today."

The two men stared at each other in silence. A lizard scuttled across the brick floor toward the cooking stones. A mouse scratched among the remains of the wedding feast.

"I will have Rachel," Jacob muttered.

The older man raised his eyebrows. "And the bride price?"

"Since you have deceived me, I consider three years of labor is long enough."

"You have dishonored me and my daughter Rachel by offering only three. As I said seven years ago, Rachel is worth ten."

"Five is all I will work."

"You worked seven for Leah. Surely Rachel would feel slighted if you labored only five for her."

Jacob's mouth became a thin line above his beard, then he bit his lower lip. "I will work seven only if I can have Rachel now."

A fair price, Laban thought. *As I planned, I'll have seven more years of hard work from my most experienced shepherd, but I can't agree yet. He made the last offer. To keep control, I must present the final one.*

Laban shaded his eyes to give the impression he was in deep thought. Slowly he lowered his hand to his beard. "You must complete the marriage week with Leah. Only then will I make the feasts for you and Rachel. In return, you will serve me an additional seven years."

"We will not bother with witnesses this time," Jacob flung at him. He stalked out of the courtyard and headed toward the pastureland.

A few minutes later Leah heard the gate open and close a second time. Her father had left to check on his flocks and his shepherds.

She went out into the courtyard. The remains of the previous day's feast littered the bricks and lay on the rugs where the men had eaten and drunk. As she watched the maidservants start to clean the courtyard, her thoughts circled in confusion. She was

Jacob's wife, but he didn't want her. No, not her—he wanted Rachel.

She would prove to Jacob that she could be a good wife, even though she was the daughter that her father had to get rid of by deceit, the one that no man wanted.

The sun was high before Rachel ventured out of Ahera's room. She spoke to no one. Without even a glance toward Leah, she went out to the pasture.

"Rachel will be happier as soon as Father talks to her," Leah explained to Zilpah.

"Why is that?"

"Father has promised her to Jacob as soon as my wedding week is complete."

The maidservant's large, dark eyes widened. "So soon? After just one week?"

"After just one week. You and Bilhah can take the midmorning meal to pasture. I don't want to see anyone."

By midafternoon Leah waited again in her room. The wedding guests had assembled to continue the week's festivities, to eat and drink with her father and Jacob, to escort Jacob again to her room. She listened to the throbbing of the harp and the beat of the tabret. The men's deep voices bragged about their wedding nights. They retold old stories—tales of other marriage feasts, narratives of family traditions, sagas of wartime.

She sat in tense anticipation. Although she longed to hold him again, she feared that he might not come or that he might refuse to touch her.

The night grew dark. The men's laughter became louder. Leah waited alone, not bothering to light the lamps. Illumination from the flickering torches in the courtyard spilled through the open door. Leaning against her clothes basket, she closed her eyes. She had deceived the man she loved and had displaced her sister. Neither Jacob nor Rachel would ever trust her again. The pain of guilt throbbed heavily in her breast.

At the sound of shouting and loud laughter from the courtyard, she glanced up. Jacob stood at her door, silhouetted against the torchlight.

"Leah," he called softly, "where are you?"

She rose quickly to her feet and reached toward him.

And so it happened each night that week. Jacob came to her, and they lay together on the sheepskins. She hoped they were making a child, a son who would look like him. This week he was hers. She would have its memory to treasure, but while he slept in her arms, she remained awake. Was she pleasing him? Did he take her only as a duty? He touched her gently, but was he thinking of Rachel?

All too soon her week was complete. Now it would be Rachel's turn to sit in the room, to listen to the wedding feast, to wait for Jacob. Leah wondered if he would ever want to come to her after he had Rachel.

Bilhah prepared the room once more as a bridal chamber. Zilpah swept the floor and Bilhah arranged oleander blossoms in pots. She laid out a new linen bridal sheet and brought cinnamon to sprinkle on the bridal bed.

"Zilpah," Leah said, "help me move my clothes basket into my stepmother's room. I want my clothes out of this room when Jacob sleeps here with Rachel. Hurry before the guests come."

"Yes, Mistress." Zilpah's soft voice revealed that the marriage plans of Rachel distressed her too.

They carried the basket and extra sheepskins across the courtyard and into Ahera's room. There the servant arranged a sleeping place for Leah.

"I'm supposed to help with the food," Zilpah said apologetically.

"Go then," Leah replied. The handmaiden walked toward the cooking fire. Leah hurried back across the courtyard to the room where she had lain each night with Jacob.

Bilhah was arranging an embroidered wedding garment over Rachel.

How beautiful my sister looks. She's especially lovely in her wedding robe. "May I help you with your necklaces?" she asked.

"Father gave me Bilhah as my wedding gift," her sister whispered. "She can dress me."

"Of course."

"I have something more to say." Leah sensed the tension in Rachel's voice.

"Yes?"

"You may have had him first, but Jacob loves me. He will really work 14 years for me."

Leah drew a sharp breath. "He may love you now, but I'll earn his love. I'm his first wife, and I'll give him his first son." She hoped her voice showed more confidence than she felt.

"You can't earn his love. He has always loved me. He kissed

me, you know, the first time he ever saw me. Did he do that to you?"

"You mean when he met you at the well? That wasn't a real kiss. It was just a greeting."

"It was a real kiss," Rachel protested. "I know. I'm the one who was there, and I'm the one he kissed. Right then I knew how he felt."

Leah shrugged. "You just fell in love with him right away. Don't forget how young and inexperienced you were. He was only kissing you in greeting and because he had just found out that you were his cousin. That kiss didn't mean anything."

"It did! It did mean something."

"You were too young to know the difference in kisses."

"How do you know?" Rachel demanded. "You've never been kissed like Jacob kissed me."

"Yes, I have," Leah blurted. Horrified, she clamped her hands over her mouth. The remainder of her uncompleted sentence burned through her mind. *Jacob kissed me that way a week ago on my wedding night when he thought I was you.*

Wheeling, she dashed from the room past the roasting lambs, the piles of fresh wheat bread, the dates and fig cakes, the jugs of wine. She stumbled into her stepmother's room and onto the bed of sheepskins. Now it was her turn to weep while her sister's marriage was consummated.

"I hope you're not going to cry all night like Rachel did." Ahera's harsh voice grated against her ears.

A sob was Leah's only answer.

"You'll have to be quiet in here," her stepmother insisted. "Rachel kept me awake all the first night and most of the rest of the week. It was horrible. I'm exhausted.

"I can't understand all these tears. You and Rachel both have what you want. So what's the problem? A man is a man. They're all alike. I could easily share mine and take some help from another woman to raise these sons."

Leah buried her face against the sheepskin.

A burst of laughter sounded from the courtyard. The guests were arriving. She heard her father's welcoming voice. She heard Jacob. She heard Teshar, the wool merchant. Soon the twang from the harp strings and the drumbeat from the tabrets reached her. The musicians' voices rose in the wedding songs.

Last week it had all been for her. She huddled into a corner. Tears streaked her face and fell silently onto the sheepskin.

Chapter 9

Leah had wept in her stepmother's room, but now in summer pasture her eyes were dry. Her hand explored the curve of her slightly rounded belly. At the same time she started out from her tent into the camp. The tent she had woven long ago and kept in the storage room all those years served as her home now. She pitched it far enough away from her sister's tent so she could avoid knowing every time Jacob went to visit Rachel. His tent and those of the shepherds completed a wide circle.

She walked out to look at the sheep and goats where they grazed on rough bunches of grass. A lamb suckled. Another leaped around its resting mother and finally jumped onto her back. A kid goat rubbed its head against Leah's leg.

"Hello, baby," she said to the goat, absentmindedly touching her own stomach again. Then she gave a little cry of delight. So gentle and so tiny she could hardly detect it, she had felt a slight movement deep inside her.

My baby, my baby! It's telling me that it's well and happy. Praise to the Lord.

As she walked slowly back, she came upon her sister watching over the sheep. Rachel glanced at Leah inquisitively. "You have a strange look on your face. What happened?"

"My baby kicked. What a wonderful feeling! You can't imagine the thrill when your baby first moves."

The younger wife looked away. "No, I can't imagine," she snapped, "because I'm not pregnant."

"I'm sorry, Rachel. I didn't mean to hurt you. I'm just so excited about the baby."

"Yes, you did mean to hurt me. You gloat over me all the

71

time because you have Jacob's baby and I don't." She turned and walked away.

Do I gloat? Leah wondered. *I don't mean to, but I suppose I do. I'm so happy because of the baby and because my child will be Jacob's firstborn. I wouldn't mind if Rachel were expecting a child too. I hope it happens soon.*

Summer transformed into early autumn. By now Leah's figure had changed to heavy fullness. The long walk from the mountain pastures back to Haran taxed her endurance.

She was glad for the month they remained in Haran before the cold winds blew down from the mountains, indicating the time had arrived to head south. Then Leah and Rachel followed Jacob and their father's flocks along the Balikh River to winter pasture.

The last day of the migration was the most tiring. At the end of the day's march, Zilpah dropped the tent down from the donkey. Together she and Leah spread it out and slipped the poles underneath in order to raise it. Leah found it hard to stoop and get up again with her bulging belly. Grasping a pole, she struggled to help her handmaiden raise the heavy tent. Even the goat-hair odor smelled stronger, more penetrating than usual. It left her feeling nauseated.

As she lifted the tent, the baby inside her kicked sharply. Leah smiled. A vigorous child this one she carried! Surely it must be a strong male child—a son for Jacob, his firstborn.

"Jacob won't hate you if you give him sons," Leah's father had told her before her marriage. "It's your duty to produce male children."

Wasn't her father always right? Jacob would love her and pay more attention to her after she delivered his son.

The tent was up, and Zilpah went out to fasten ropes. Cramping drove Leah to grab her abdomen with both hands.

"Zilpah!"

The servant woman peered into the tent. "What is it, Mistress?"

"I had a pain. Do you think the baby is coming?"

"The time is right. Let me put down a sheepskin for you to lie on so I can examine you."

Zilpah's steady fingers explored the outline of the baby. "It's in a good position," she reported, "with its head well down."

Leah winced in pain again.

"Rest while you can," Zilpah advised. "You've been walking all day. I'll fasten the tent ropes and bring in the rugs and the rest of the sheepskins. First I'd better send Bilhah to look for the right-sized stones that we need for a birthing stool."

What did Leah hear in the woman's voice? Excitement? Nervousness? Fear? Or did she imagine she heard them because they were her own feelings?

Leah went out and sat down on a pile of sheepskins. Overhead the gray winter sky seemed to press down on her. She had hurried to put up her tent before the afternoon rain. Now the first large drops splashed onto her head scarf. Staggering slightly, she got up to enter the tent.

Zilpah had unrolled the woven rugs, covering the earth inside the tent except for one section. She left that bare for the birthing stones. "Lie down now," she told Leah. She hurried to arrange additional sheepskins into a resting place for her mistress. Using sparks from flint and pyrite, she lit a fire in the brazier.

The tent shuddered from a burst of wind and a shower of rain. The day darkened although night had not yet fallen. Zilpah lit lamps from the brazier fire. Leah squinted to watch her arrange cushions and bolsters.

Bilhah dragged in a stone and left it on the bare section of ground. Soon she brought the second one and placed it alongside the other, leaving a space between.

The stones stood about a hand high and were just big enough for a woman to sit on as a birthing stool. Leah watched Zilpah line the space between the stones with a generous supply of sheep's wool, thick and soft, in case the baby should slip from her grasp. She padded the tops of the stones with pieces of sheepskin.

Again wind gusted against the tent. Was the storm god angry with her? Would something evil happen to her baby? She visualized the deity's fierce figure. The storm god stood on a snarling bronze panther. No! No! He was powerless. Hadn't she given up the worship of such gods? She tried to push the image out of her mind, reminding herself that Jacob said if she trusted in the Lord, the storm god could hold no control over her. Still, her father had always told her that the storm god could send destruction.

"Do you think my baby will be all right?" she asked anxiously.

Zilpah washed her flushed face with a damp cloth. "You're

healthy and I find no problem for the delivery that could possibly harm the baby."

"More pain," Leah gasped. "Harder. Send someone to tell Jacob that his child is on the way. He has the right to know."

The servant woman slipped out, and Leah heard her call to a shepherd boy. The voice of a shepherd's wife rose in excited exclamation. The news would spread rapidly.

A heavy ache filled the small of Leah's back. It hurt to move, yet she couldn't lie still when the pains came. She pushed her damp hair away from her face, then clenched her fists to fight the pain.

Fingers touched the back of her neck, rubbing something slippery—Zilpah, soothing the tension with aloe gel.

"Relax your hands, Mistress. Take deep breaths."

"I'll try," she whispered.

How unreal it was! Other women gave birth, but she was Leah, the daughter that no man had wanted to marry.

"Jacob, Jacob," she screamed although she knew that he was far away in the fields with the sheep. *Jacob, I may be weak-eyed, but I'm strong enough to give you your firstborn.*

The wind continued to lash the tent, but the palm-fiber ropes held it steady.

Zilpah put a cup to her lips. "Sip a bit of this. It will ease the pain a little." Leah could swallow only a mouthful of the bitter herbal tincture.

"We're going to put you on the birthing stool now," the servant woman announced. Leah fought against dizziness and nausea as the maids helped her to the covered stones. The sheepskin padding was warm against her bare skin.

She was aware that Zilpah knelt in front of her. Bilhah sat behind her. Leah felt Bilhah slip her arms around and lock her hands firmly above her belly, ready to help push.

Will I give birth to a son? Will he be all right? She moaned. Would the pain never stop? The downward pressure intensified. Suddenly the baby's head emerged.

"Push! Push the baby out," Zilpah commanded.

Leah strained, rising slightly from the stones. The baby slid into Zilpah's waiting hands. "A son!" she exclaimed. "You've given birth to a male child."

Quickly she held the infant upside down, letting the mucus run out of his mouth. He fought for breath and filled his lungs. His angry cry rang through the tent. Tears rolled down Leah's face, relief and joy mingling. She had produced a son for Jacob.

Zilpah placed the baby on Leah's knees. Light from the lamps and the brazier glinted off the flint knife that she used to cut the umbilical cord. She handed the crying infant to Bilhah and turned her attention to Leah, wrapping the bloody after-birth in the thick fleece she had placed earlier between the stones.

"Where's my baby?" Leah struggled to speak. "I want to hold him."

"Bilhah is cleaning him with olive oil. As soon as she rubs him with salt to toughen his skin, she'll bring him to you."

"I want to hold him now."

"First I have to take care of you. I want you to look nice when Master Jacob comes." Zilpah led her to the sheepskin bed and helped her pull on a clean tunic. Then she propped her against bolsters and pillows and combed her hair with gentle strokes.

"What do you think Jacob will say when he finds out I've produced a son for him?" Leah asked, her voice tinged with exhaustion. Another question she left unspoken. *Will he tell me that he loves me?*

Bilhah brought the infant. She had wrapped him securely in soft, woolen swaddling clothes.

"My son," Leah whispered to him. Putting him under the robe that covered her, she pressed his warm head next to her cheek. His dark hair was still damp and he smelled like olive oil. She kissed his red face while he made little sucking noises with his mouth.

The tent flap opened, letting in a drift of cold air. Jacob entered.

Leah pulled back the robe to show the baby. "Look. You have a son," she announced proudly.

"Is he strong and healthy?"

"Strong like his father."

"You have done well with the seed I planted. What would you like to name him?"

"I would like to call him Reuben," she offered shyly.

Jacob nodded. "Eight days from now when I circumcise him, I will name him Reuben."

Leah shuddered. The thought of the knife cutting into her baby's flesh sent a shiver through her. "Do you have to circumcise him?"

"Of course I have to circumcise him. It's the sign of our covenant with the Lord. He'll cry a little when I cut away the skin, but when he's grown into manhood, he'll be proud of this mark on his body. The Lord gave us the sign. It shows that we are His people and that He has promised us the land."

Jacob touched the infant's cheek with his finger. Then he spoke the ritual words, "I accept you as my firstborn."

Leah yearned to say, "I love you, Jacob. Out of my love I have guarded your seed and I have produced this firstborn son for you." But something held the words within her. What was it? Why couldn't she tell him? Instead she murmured, "Thank you for accepting him."

Stroking the baby's cheek again, he said as if no one was listening. "Why didn't Rachel give me my firstborn son?" With that he left. The tent flap fell behind him.

Now Leah knew why she hesitated to tell him of her deep love. Couldn't he love her, the mother of his son, as well as loving Rachel? Why couldn't he care for both of them? Why couldn't he give her at least a part of his love?

Outside the wind no longer gusted. Instead, rain droned steadily on the top of the tent.

Chapter 10

The design in the woolen cloth blurred into an indistinct pattern. Leah leaned away from the portable loom and laid the shuttle on her lap. She held both hands to her head to still the dizzy swirling.

How thankful she was that her father and Jacob were not moving the flocks this day. Spring rains had provided good mountain pasture. The sheep and goats would graze for longer than usual at this resting place.

In spite of the dizzy spell, Leah smiled. She was pregnant. Even though she still nursed Reuben, the Lord had blessed her. Raising her head toward the blue sky, she murmured, "Thank You, Lord, God of Jacob."

"Are you expecting another baby?" Rachel demanded from behind her.

"I think so."

"You just think so?"

"No, I'm sure."

"That's two for you and none for me. It's not fair."

Leah threw the shuttle through the warp on the loom. "Jacob comes to me only when you have your monthly sickness. He spends more time in your tent than he does in mine. I can't help that you're not pregnant."

"Just because you're jealous of me," Rachel retorted, "just because Jacob loves me and doesn't love you, does that mean you have to be so smug?"

"Smug? I'm not smug," her sister protested, knowing full well that she felt she had the right to the children since Rachel claimed all of their husband's love. Immediately guilt overwhelmed her. Her fingers tugged at the threads of her weaving. This was Rachel, her sister—her little sister—the child she had raised, the young woman who deserved a baby as much as she.

Leah turned to speak to Rachel, but her sister had gone. She was walking back to the pasture where she helped Jacob with the sheep and goats.

As the months passed, as her belly grew larger, Leah tried to avoid Rachel's envious glances.

In due season after they had gone south to pasture, while a cold winter wind blew out of the north and rattled against the tent, Leah gave birth.

"Another son," Zilpah announced. She handed the baby to Bilhah to cleanse him.

"A son," Leah whispered to herself from the birthing stones. "The Lord has heard my prayer."

Rachel entered the tent. "I heard the baby cry." She looked down at the newborn child, red and wrinkled. "I see it's another boy."

"Another son for Jacob," Leah said as Zilpah helped her from the stones to the sheepskin bed.

"What will you name him?" Rachel asked impassively.

Leah spoke with effort. "Jacob still hates me for deceiving him on the wedding night, but the Lord has heard my call to Him. He has answered my prayer for another son. I'll name him Simeon, 'He heard.' "

Suddenly Rachel glanced wildly around—at the baby, at Leah, at Zilpah and Bilhah. Her voice burst out in anguish. "I've called to the God of Jacob and I've called to Father's gods. None have heard me. I have no answer. I have no son."

She rushed out into the darkness.

"Rachel, wait!" Leah cried after her.

Only the moan of the cold north wind blowing against the door flap answered her.

Before the caravan left winter pasture for Haran, Leah was pregnant again. When the time came to migrate to home pasture, Leah wrapped Simeon in a long woolen shawl. She circled the shawl around herself, binding her baby close against her breast, warm against her body.

Zilpah carried Reuben as they trudged slowly north. Together the women drove the donkeys and kept watch over the milk goats. Leah needed the milk for Reuben and soon would need it for Simeon also.

Shepherds trudged along the sides of the flocks to prevent

the animals from straying. Leah could make out the figures of Jacob and Rachel walking together—always together those two.

Just ahead, close behind the flocks, her stepmother Ahera rode on a camel with her youngest son sitting behind her. Her two maidservants walked on one side. Since Ahera was unaccustomed to traveling long distances in the annual migration, Laban had bought the mount for her. He too rode one at the head of his flocks.

Leah plodded slowly along behind the donkeys and goats, trying unsuccessfully to overcome her resentment of Ahera. Simeon weighed heavily in Leah's arms. Waves of nausea attacked her. "I would appreciate a camel to ride on right now," she remarked to Zilpah.

Zilpah shifted Reuben to her other hip and muttered in agreement, "These babies are heavy to carry."

The second night of the migration to Haran, Leah as usual tended the cooking fire. After working to separate the sheep and goats for the night, Rachel and Jacob came from the field to eat the evening meal.

A short distance away Laban sat by his wife's cooking fire and wished he were at Leah's. Not only was his daughter a better cook, but she took an interest in the flocks. Rachel too ate at Leah's fire, and since she was a shepherdess, she could converse with knowledge about sheep and goats.

Ahera knew nothing about animals and refused to learn. Laban's sons were still too young to talk intelligently with him about shepherding.

He glanced toward his older daughter's tent. The aroma of a savory stew cooking over her fire drifted his way. He saw Leah remove the pot from the coals and pour some of the stew into a bowl for Jacob to eat.

Laban never trusted his son-in-law completely, but he had to admit to himself that he enjoyed talking to him. He thought back to the time before he had taken Ahera for his wife, to the evenings when he and Jacob had eaten together and then talked long and leisurely by Leah's fire.

He glanced down at the garbanzo beans on his flatbread. His evening meal lacked the herbs and spices that she put into her cooking.

When he looked up again, Jacob was walking toward him. Laban pointed to a rug on the ground. "The flocks are increasing considerably this spring," his nephew observed.

Laban nodded in satisfaction. "We have a good number of ewes that are lambing for the first time."

"That means we need more help to watch over the sheep. Too many new lambs could easily stray or be taken by bears or wolves or hyenas in summer pasture."

"That means I should hire more shepherds or buy more slaves," Laban said after considering the problem a moment. "This will be expensive."

"Not necessarily. You could use dogs."

"Dogs!" Laban shouted, clenching his fists. "I would never allow dogs to come near my flocks."

Jacob drew back from the anger in his voice. "Sheepmen in Canaan use dogs to help herd the flocks. You could ask a caravan leader to bring some up here to Haran. If you order them right away, you might have them before we leave for summer pasture."

"Never!" Laban stood and stared out toward the pasture. "Dogs are enemies of sheep. I could lose all my lambs to a pack of dogs."

"Sheep dogs don't run in wild packs," Jacob said, also rising. "It's true that dogs are instinctively the enemy of sheep, but sheep dogs are trained to guard the animals against attack."

"An alert shepherd can guard 50 to 100 sheep," Laban said disdainfully. "Who needs dogs?"

"With a couple of dogs a shepherd can watch over more than 300. You could cut your expenses way down."

Laban turned Jacob's argument over in his mind. Could dogs really save him money? "How can anyone teach a dog to overcome its instinct to murder sheep and goats?" he asked.

"They are trained to go only so far with their hunt-and-kill instinct when herding the sheep."

Unconvinced, Laban muttered, "I don't believe it. Too many times I've lost sheep and goats to dogs. I'll never bring them near my flocks."

"I see we can't come to agreement," Jacob said tersely. He headed back to Leah's fire.

Laban watched him walk away. More and more he and his nephew disagreed on matters of business. Jacob was changing, growing restless, talking more about Canaan. Probably he was counting the time until he could return to his homeland. When he did, Laban would lose his best sheepman—and his daughters.

The remains of his flatbread and garbanzo beans were cold. He tossed them into the fire. Aching shoulder muscles reminded him that he was growing older. It was no time of life to lose his family.

Jacob sat down near Rachel, reached out and touched her shoulder.

She drew away from him, muttering, "Leah's pregnant again."

"So?"

"Why can't you do the same for me?"

"I do the planting. It's up to you to hold onto the seed."

With a sob she ran to her tent.

Months later during a stormy night, Zilpah held up Leah's slippery newborn. "It's a boy."

"Another son," Leah gasped happily. She groaned with each contraction that expelled the afterbirth into the space between the birthing stones. Later she lay comfortably on her sheepskin bed. Zilpah brought her the baby.

"Three sons," Leah said. "Now Jacob will really consider me his wife. He'll be joined to me at last. In celebration I'll call this son Levi."

"What does the name mean?" Zilpah asked.

"It means 'attachment.' I hope Jacob will approve of my choice."

When morning dawned, Leah stiffened in nervous anticipation of his visit to inspect his new son. As soon as he opened the tent flap, she pulled back her robe to show him the sleeping infant. "Another son for you."

"Another son," he echoed with satisfaction. "Have you thought of a name for him?"

"I would like to call him Levi because it means 'attachment.' "

"Levi." Jacob considered the name. "Levi, you have become attached to your family." He leaned down and touched the baby's forehead. "I accept you."

Leah felt her throat muscles tighten. Of course she was happy that Jacob was pleased with his son, but she had hoped for an attachment of Jacob to her. With effort she managed to say "Thank you" before he left.

On her bed she turned to face the dark wall of the tent. Her husband saw her only as a successful carrier of his seed. She wanted him to love her as a wife, to love her the way he did Rachel! Closing her eyes, she tried to hold onto her flickering hope of Jacob's love. The tiny flame threatened to go out completely.

Levi opened his eyes and started to cry lustily. His tiny face turned dark red in frustration. Already he was demanding food. Leah turned her attention away from her own need and met that of Jacob's son.

Now Reuben was old enough to ride on a donkey for the trip from winter pasture to Haran. His mother strapped storage baskets onto the donkey and padded its back with a sheepskin. She lifted the child onto the sheepskin.

Zilpah carried Simeon. Leah wrapped Levi closely against her. Already she detected the swelling of her body that indicated that the next baby was on its way.

The long trip taxed her strength. She sighed in relief when at last she could pitch her tent in the pastureland near Haran.

Their provisions were low. The following morning Leah strapped two large baskets onto a donkey and headed for the city marketplace.

Near South Gate she noticed a merchant's caravan, the camels resting on the hard-packed ground. The men had removed the heavy packs and were laying out the merchandise on colorful rugs. Jars of almond oil, linen and cotton cloth, and expensive blue dye told Leah that the caravan had traveled all the way from Egypt. Other rugs held ivory combs, spoons, bottles, and boxes. Fine bronze lamps and silver cups indicated that the leader had stopped the caravan at Damascus to trade for its unique metalware.

Leah passed the caravan and entered South Gate. She slowed as she considered a visit with her stepmother. No, not today. A visit to her father's house always distressed her—the unswept courtyard, her three half-brothers with runny noses and grimy faces. She knew that his wife's inability to manage the household annoyed her father.

Leah drove the donkey toward the food market.

Two hours later, with her baskets filled with wheat, barley, dried apricots, jugs of pickled olives and sesame oil, fresh coriander and fresh parsley, Leah left the city. As she passed the resting camels, the caravan leader intercepted her. "You are Leah, the daughter of Laban the sheepman?"

"Yes, I am."

"You are also the first wife of Jacob, Laban's nephew from Canaan?"

"This is true."

"I have a message for your father and for your husband from Isaac the sheepman in Beersheba."

They didn't often receive a message from a distant land. Her heart skipped in excitement. "You will find my father and my husband in the pastureland."

"I haven't any time to go so far. As you can see, the shopkeepers are already arriving from the city to buy my merchandise. It's impossible for me to leave. Since you are Laban's first daughter and Jacob's first wife, I'll entrust you with the message for them."

"And what news do you bring?"

"I know few details." The caravan leader paused. "I know only that Laban's sister Rebekah, who is Jacob's mother, has died."

"Oh!" Leah's hand flew to cover her mouth.

The merchant continued "Her people buried her east of Mamre. That's the burial cave that Jacob's ancestor Abraham bought."

Leah lashed the back of the donkey with her willow switch. "I must hurry to tell my father and my husband."

She felt relieved to find her father before she found her husband. He stood in the pasture. A newborn lamb, still wet, tottered by his feet.

"Father, a caravan leader brought news from Beersheba." As gently as she could, she told him. They sat down on a rock, her head on his sagging shoulder.

"I must inform Jacob," he said at last. He got heavily to his feet and crossed the field.

Leah waited anxiously for Jacob to return for the evening meal. The night grew dark and he didn't come. She and Rachel sat by the fire and spoke in hushed voices. They had never known their aunt Rebekah, but still they felt a deep sadness at the loss of their only kinswoman.

Early in the morning Leah set out to find her husband. Dark clouds, driven by a cool, brisk wind out of the northwest, hurried across the sky. She drew her woolen shawl closely around her shoulders and sheltered her hands in its folds.

The sheep scattered before her as she pushed her way

through the flock in her search for Jacob. At last she saw him seated on a flat stone. Hesitantly she approached him.

"I accompany you in your sorrow." She recited the customary words of sympathy.

He remained silent, staring at the leather sandals that protected his feet.

She longed to sit next to him and rest her head on his shoulder as she had done to her father. Together they could share their grief.

Did he recognize her presence? He gave no sign of it. She touched him lightly on the arm. Still no response. His sorrow he bore entirely within himself.

Slowly she returned to the camp. Then she and Rachel sat together in Leah's tent. There they lifted the death wail, a thin cry that undulated—at times rising to a high-pitched lament—at times descending to a low moan. Wind carried the wailing down into the flocks. The ewes and rams raised their heads, questioning the unaccustomed sound.

Months later the camp was well settled into winter pasture before Leah felt the first pangs of impending childbirth. She had slept restlessly most of the night until a contraction startled her into instant wakefulness. She sat up.

"Zilpah!" she called through the woven drapery that separated her portion of the tent from that of her maidservant.

The woman rushed in and knelt at her side. "Did you feel a pain?"

"A strong one. I think this birth won't take long."

"The birthing stones are ready. Let me feel how far down the baby has dropped."

With experienced fingers Zilpah ran her hands over Leah's body where it protected the unborn child.

"Another strong one," Leah groaned as the contraction seized her.

"I'll get Bilhah and we'll put you on the birthing stones right away." Zilpah raced to Rachel's tent.

"Hurry!" Leah gasped after her. She stared out through the tent opening. A bright light hung near the horizon. The morning star. Even with Leah's dim vision, the star was bright enough for her to see. The morning star—a good sign for this child's birth.

She lay down to wait for Zilpah and Bilhah, but the baby would not wait. In a rush of water he emerged. Quickly Leah held him upside down to allow mucus to run out of his nose and mouth. The infant sucked in a breath and let out a lusty cry.

Zilpah and Bilhah ran into the tent. "Oh, Mistress!" Zilpah exclaimed.

"He came so fast," Leah told her. Bilhah took the crying infant from her arms.

After Bilhah had cared for the newborn, she brought him to Leah. The morning light revealed his dark eyes and the thick black hair that covered his head. It extended like a mane down the back of his neck.

Leah held him close to her breast. She loved the smell of his newness—the olive oil, the salt, the dampness in his hair. She kissed the top of his head. "Praise to the Lord, the God of Jacob—my God too. Dear baby, I will name you Judah, 'praise.' "

When Zilpah returned from burying the afterbirth, Leah said, "Jacob took his turn watching the flocks during the night. Send someone to tell him he has a new son."

Four sons for Jacob. Leah tensed as she wondered once more about his reaction to his newest child. Always she hoped he might say he loved her for carrying another son, yet she really no longer expected to her the words.

Jacob leaned down to examine his son. "Ai!" he exclaimed, "you have done well with this one, Leah. See the mane down his neck. He looks like a lion's cub."

"I would like to name him Judah, praise to the Lord."

"He shall be Judah." Her husband laid his hand for a moment on his new son's head. "Rachel can't hold on to the seed I plant, but Leah, you carry it well." Then he was gone, back to the flock.

"Judah, Judah, praise to the Lord," she repeated. "You have pleased your father. You are a special son, already a favored child, little lion's cub." She kissed his warm, red cheek. "I've always hoped your father would love me like he loves Rachel, but I have one happiness in knowing he loves his sons."

Rachel arrived, her dark eyes pools of misery. "You have four and I have none. But I will have children. I will. I will, I'll give Bilhah to Jacob to bear sons for me, but they will be mine. Mine!"

Leah knew what Bilhah's help would mean. Law in Haran allowed a married woman to give her slave woman to her husband. Any babies born to the slave would belong to the wife.

One more glance at the newborn child and Rachel hurried out of the tent.

Tears splashed onto Judah's head—tears of sympathy for her sister's pain, tears of fear.

If Rachel had children, her sons would become Jacob's favorites, displacing Judah and the others. When her sister with Bilhah's aid produced sons, Leah's slender hold on Jacob would disappear. He would need her no longer and might cast her aside. The painful memory of the words he had flung at her father long ago rose up in her mind. "Couldn't you get rid of her any other way?"

Chapter 11

Bilhah is having a hard time putting up Mistress Rachel's tent," Zilpah said. "Shall I help her?"

Of course the servant woman was having trouble. Leah knew the difficulty of pitching a tent when a woman had only three or four full moons to go before giving birth.

She turned away and stared across the home pasture. The maidservant's rounded abdomen reminded Leah all too vividly that she was not pregnant. Rachel's maid now carried Jacob's seed.

"Four sons," Leah said to Zilpah after the woman had securely pitched Rachel's tent. "Why did the Lord bless me with four sons and then stop? Why doesn't He let me have more?"

"They don't sound like a blessing right now. I think Simeon and Levi are fighting again."

Leah left the cooking fire and went to the entrance to the tent. Two of her small sons had piled cushions and bolsters into a mound. They had been jumping on them, but now Simeon was kicking his brother. Judah slept peacefully on sheepskins in spite of the commotion going on near him.

"Hush," she warned, "you'll wake up Judah."

"Levi bit me," Simeon shouted.

Leah pulled him away from his younger brother. "Stop fighting and go outside to play."

Simeon shuffled out of the tent, and Levi toddled after him. Judah stirred slightly but continued to sleep.

"Zilpah, come into the tent. I need to talk to you."

The woman entered. "Yes, Mistress."

Nervously Leah brushed back her long hair and rubbed the side of her face. "Remember how happy I was when Reuben was born. I was sure Jacob would love me when I gave him his firstborn son. I hoped again when Simeon was born."

"Then you gave him Levi and Judah."

"I hoped after each one, but now my hope has grown thin. I used to think I could earn Jacob's love by giving him sons. It didn't turn out that way."

Zilpah glanced over to the sheepskins where Judah still slept. She picked up a couple of cushions from where Simeon and Levi had piled them and dropped them in their proper places by the wall. "You mustn't give up hope. Remember how pleased Master Jacob was when Judah was born."

Leah smiled when she thought of the dark-eyed child's birth—and easy labor with him.

Leah picked up a cushion to help Zilpah arrange the tent. "Yes, Jacob was pleased with Judah," she agreed, "but how can I please him again when I'm not even expecting a child?" She took a deep breath and the words tumbled out. "I can't even hope that my husband will love me unless I'm producing sons."

"Maybe after the next full moon you'll find that you're pregnant again."

"I can't take that chance. I'll have to give Jacob more sons. You know Bilhah is pregnant. She's the one carrying Jacob's seed." Leah shook her head. "I should be the one—or Rachel, of course, but it's not happening. If Bilhah can do it, so can you, Zilpah. I'm giving you to Jacob."

"Oh, Mistress Leah!" She pressed her hands to her face.

"Yes, you must give me another son."

Zilpah said nothing. Only a low moan escaped her throat.

Leah's voice was subdued. "You know how important it is for me to give Jacob sons so he will love me."

"Yes, Mistress."

Judah turned over and opened his eyes. He started to whimper. Leah picked him up and held him against her shoulder. She kissed the side of his head. His dark hair, slightly damp, felt comforting under her lips.

"Zilpah, finish baking the bread." Leah tried to hide her pangs of uneasiness. "I'm going to the fields to speak to Jacob. Here, keep Judah with you." She handed the infant to her servant.

Leah wandered among the sheep, unsure where to find her husband. Some of the sheep were grazing up a sunny slope. They scattered as she headed for the top. A shepherd sat in the shade of a scrubby bush, playing a solitary game with some stones as he watched over the animals nearest him.

"Have you seen Master Jacob?"

"I can see him from here." He pointed across the field. Leah walked in the direction he indicated. How should she begin? Would he take Zilpah willingly?

At last she saw her husband where he quietly watched the flock. She was able to approach quite close before he glanced up. "You surprised me," he said.

"I have something important to discuss with you," she said, seating herself on a stone opposite him. She took a deep breath. "Reuben is your firstborn son. Then we had Simeon and Levi and Judah."

"I know who my sons are."

"Four sons are not enough."

"You women want more and more sons," he said in a low voice. "If they don't come, you blame me."

"I'm not blaming you, but—"

"I plant the seed," he broke in. "I do my part. It's the woman's job to carry the seed and produce the baby. Rachel claims it's my fault that she can't carry a child."

"I'm not blaming you," she repeated softly, "but you want more sons, too, don't you?"

Jacob gazed across the field. "Of course I want more sons. It's only natural for a man to want many sons to carry on his traditions and to take care of him in his old age."

Leah's voice trembled slightly. "Take my maidservant Zilpah to have more sons."

"Why can't you give them to me?" he demanded. "Why do I have to take Zilpah? I took Bilhah because Rachel can't hold any of the seed I plant. But you have. You've done it before. Why do I have to take Zilpah? I see no reason why you can't produce more sons for me." He paused before he added wistfully, "I've always depended upon you."

"I don't know why I can't." She felt desperate. "I don't know why. It's just not happening. I can't see any way to have more sons unless I give Zilpah to you."

"If that's the only way—all right. I'll take her," he grumbled. "Just leave me some peace and quiet."

She started to return to the camp.

"Wait," he called.

She went back to him. Had he changed his mind already?

He cleared his throat. "We must thank the Lord for the sons we have and ask His good fortune to stay with us."

Taking her by the hand, he led her slightly away from the sheep. They stood side by side in the field and raised their faces toward the sky. His hand around hers felt warm and strong.

After a few moments of silence he prayed, "Thank You, Lord, for the sons You have given me—Reuben, the firstborn, a fine young lad—for Simeon and Levi, healthy and full of energy—for Judah, a sturdy little lion's cub. Do not forsake us, Lord. Send us Your good fortune."

Then he was silent again, listening for any message the Lord might wish to send. A soft breeze blew across the land. It touched Leah's face like a caress. She heard the familiar sound of bleating sheep, felt the vibrations of their hooves on earth, smelled the oily aroma of warm sunshine on wool.

I love you, Jacob, filled her mind, edging out the prayer of thanksgiving for their sons. *Why can't I bring myself to tell you that I love you?*

His voice broke the closeness of the moment. "I'll go to Zilpah tonight."

The shock of his words stabbed like a knife in her heart. What had she done? Was having more sons worth the jealousy that was already mounting and which threatened to throw her into panic? She smiled weakly at Jacob and left him to his contemplation in the pasture.

As Leah made her way back to the tent, she stumbled over a rock in the path. She caught herself from falling and stood completely still. A harsh realization hit her. Zilpah's small section of the tent was immediately to the side of Leah's larger one. Only a drapery, woven from wool, divided the two rooms. Leah would be able to hear everything. In deep thought she walked the remaining distance to the camp.

Zilpah was scooping dry sheep dung from a basket onto the fire.

"Jacob will come to you tonight," Leah informed her brusquely.

The servant woman turned her head away, but not quickly enough. Leah saw her fleeting smile.

As Leah went through the routines of preparing the evening meal, she felt a tension between herself and her maidservant. They had always worked well together, preparing the food, setting up the tent, caring for the children. Now Zilpah avoided looking at her. In a few hours the loyal maidservant and trusted friend had become another rival.

Jacob came from the pasture to eat boiled lamb and barley stew. After he finished eating, Leah saw him glance sideways at Zilpah. He ran his lean brown hand down his beard. Zilpah avoided his gaze, but the smile on her lips was clearly evident.

For the first time in her life Leah wished the sun would hold still, that night would never come. Instead, across the flat pastureland the sun sank below the horizon and night settled quickly.

Reuben, Simeon, and Levi slept on their sheepskins near Leah. She lay in the darkness of the tent with Judah sucking contentedly at her breast. Through the woven drapery sounds came from Zilpah's room—Jacob lifting the side of the tent to enter, Zilpah's giggling laugh, his deep whisper.

Leah wiped the perspiration from her face with a corner of her sleeping robe. Judah had fallen asleep with his mouth still on her breast. She moved him gently aside and lay quietly to avoid disturbing him. Sleep refused to come to her, however. She heard the night sounds, heard Jacob breathing in deep sleep. Levi stirred on his sheepskin. In a nearby tent a shepherd child coughed. Out by the fire field mice rustled as they searched for drops of barley. A restless goat wandered near the tent to tug on the twigs of a bush.

Although Leah held her body as still as possible, her mind raced. She would have to find another place for Zilpah to sleep. Listening to her husband in bed with another woman was too hard to bear. While she could order Zilpah to weave a tent, that would require many weeks of work. Where could she find a tent? Then she remembered a very old one—her grandfather's tent. When she was a child, her mother had kept it stored in the lean-to as a remembrance of her parents. Where was it now? Leah would ask her father.

The sun came up and still she had not slept. She was nursing Judah when she heard Jacob leave. Holding Judah on one hip, Leah went out to tend the morning fire.

Zilpah came around the side of the tent. Although she had combed her hair, it had a tousled look. Her eyes shone with an abnormal brightness and her tan cheeks held an unusual redness.

The two women worked side by side. Zilpah shook a goatskin filled with fermented goat milk that was at the right consistency to turn into cheese. Leah laid Judah on a rug and then set a pot of lentils on the fire to boil. She placed handfuls of ground wheat into another bowl and added salt and water to make dough for flatbread.

The servant woman laid the skin of goat milk aside. "Let me make the bread," she offered. "You look tired."

Of course I'm tired, Leah thought, *but I won't admit it to you.* "I can do it myself."

At midmorning she left Zilpah with the children. She loaded a basket with enough food for Jacob and Rachel and for her father. Long ago Ahera had agreed that Leah could provide the midmorning meal for Laban.

In the field Leah waited impatiently while her father and her husband ate, not daring to raise her eyes to look at Jacob. Later, while Rachel ate, Leah followed Laban to where he watched his shepherds.

"Father," she greeted him, "may I ask a question?"

"You may ask."

"Do you remember my grandfather's tent? When I was a child, Mother kept it in the lean-to. We never used it because it was too old."

"I remember it. Why do you ask?"

"If you still have it, will you give it to me?"

"Why would you want that old tent?"

In a choking voice Leah explained, "I've given Zilpah to Jacob. I want a tent for her."

"You have four sons. Isn't that enough? That's more than Ahera has done for me. You've done well, Leah. Can't you leave well enough alone?"

"Rachel gave Bilhah to Jacob."

"And so you think Rachel will get ahead of you?"

"Jacob loves Rachel. He'll never love me if I don't continue to give him sons."

"Leah, Leah." His voice softened. "You never give up hope, do you? If you want it, you may have the tent for Zilpah. Take a donkey to carry it. Old Narum uses it for padding under his sheepskins, but I'll have Ahera give him extra sheepskins to sleep on. You may have the tent."

It was afternoon by the time Leah wearily drove the loaded donkey back to camp. The sleepless night had left her exhausted.

"Zilpah," she called, "here's a tent for you. Pitch it on the other side of Rachel's."

At the sight of it, the woman's eyes widened and her mouth twitched as she tried to hide another smile. She led the donkey beyond Rachel's tent.

Leah watched for a moment, then with a deep sigh turned her attention to her four sons.

As they sat together in the dirt Simeon hit Levi, and he let out a loud yell. From inside the tent Judah screamed for food. Reuben crouched by the fire, poking a stick into the coals.

Chapter 12

Even though Zilpah pitched her tent on the other side of Rachel's, Leah knew which nights Jacob slept with the maidservant. The glances between the two in the early evening told her. She knew because of Zilpah's face in the morning—first an expression that boasted, "Jacob came to my tent," followed by another look that begged, "Forgive me, Mistress."

Leah wished she could take back her decision to give Zilpah to Jacob, but it was too late. She glanced toward the cooking fire where Zilpah squatted to stir the pot of simmering bean-and-barley stew. Already her belly was starting to round.

The child would belong to Leah, of course. Zilpah would sit on the birthing stones, and Bilhah would deliver the child. She would place the baby directly on Leah's knees, and in that moment it would become her child. It was the law and the custom.

Leah wondered if another son would be worth the anguish she had already endured. Knowing Jacob went to Rachel and to Bilhah had been hard enough, but then at her own suggestion he had taken Zilpah, her trusted maidservant. The sight of Zilpah's thickening figure forced Leah into constant awareness that the maidservant was carrying her husband's seed.

Assured of Zilpah's pregnancy, Jacob turned his attention to Rachel again. Leah waited for him to come to her, but weeks passed, then months.

Simeon and Levi dashed past Leah. As he tried to catch his brother, Levi sprawled onto the rocky dirt and howled loudly. Leah picked him up and eased his tears with kisses. She carried him into the tent and rocked him back and forth in her arms.

Was her father right? Were four sons enough? Even though

the law said she could give her maidservant to her husband and the children would belong to her, she wondered about the wisdom of what she had done.

Levi stopped crying and fell asleep on her shoulder. She laid him gently onto a sheepskin and started toward the tent entrance.

Rachel came from her fire, carrying Dan, the baby Bilhah had borne for her. She kissed his neck and he squealed and laughed in delight. "Zilpah is already starting to show," she remarked.

Leah glanced over to where Zilpah sat by the fire. "I think she sticks out her belly on purpose."

"Aren't you pleased? I thought you wanted more children."

"Of course I want more children. I wouldn't have given her to him if I hadn't wanted more children."

Rachel shifted Dan from one shoulder to the other. "Then why are you unhappy?"

"I don't know." Leah turned away from Rachel. She knew why she was unhappy, but she refused to discuss it with her sister. Rachel monopolized their husband's affection. He had no time for Leah, and by giving Zilpah to Jacob she had lost her maidservant's friendship. She had no one with whom she could share her concerns and fears and hopes. So—what else could go wrong?

"You might like to know that Bilhah is expecting another baby too."

"Oh!" Leah sat down on a rug. Both maids pregnant at the same time—this was too much.

Dan nuzzled against Rachel's breast, searching for milk. "I'll have to take him to Bilhah now." She sauntered back to her tent.

By Leah's fire Zilpah stirred the stew again. In a few months she would give birth. If Leah had good luck, she would have a new son, a reward for all her misery. She would name him Gad, "good fortune." Although she had lost a trusted friend, she would gain a son.

"The baby is kicking," Zilpah called to her. "He's strong already. I think he'll grow up to become a great warrior."

Leah said nothing. Naturally the woman would prefer this baby, but Leah would always favor Judah and Reuben. Judah was a charming child with a warm and loving personality—a child to hug when she felt in need of reassurance.

As for Reuben, she found herself depending often on his help to watch over the younger boys, to run errands for her, and to identify objects and persons she couldn't distinguish from a distance.

Zilpah didn't appear to notice that her mistress had remained silent.

"Stay with the children," Leah told her. "I'm going to walk into Haran. Reuben needs a new robe, and I haven't had time to weave one for him. We're almost out of spices, too."

Leah took a basket and headed for the city. She felt a need for solitude, a time to think through what was happening to her. The trip to market for spices and a length of cloth was an excuse to have some time to herself. As she strolled along the road to Haran, sheep and goats grazed in the fields on short bunches of grass.

No child, she thought, *no child on the way.* Leah had been sure she could earn his love by producing sons. But for the past months Jacob had spent most of his nights in Rachel's tent. The Lord had given her loving children, but withheld the love of her husband.

She stopped. Really she felt she didn't have a husband. Jacob was the father of her sons, but he denied her the respect and love due to a first wife.

The pastureland ended abruptly, and now ripe wheat fields lined the sides of the road. A group of farm workers walked toward her, harvesting knives in their hands. They looked the other way instead of greeting her. At wheat harvest time the farmers were especially belligerent and surly to shepherds and their families. How many times had she heard them shout, "Keep those sheep and goats out of our fields or we'll get you for the damage the do."

The walls of Haran rose in front of her. She passed through South Gate. After a few minutes she turned into a crooked street that led to the food market.

In the market she shouldered her way through the crowd of shoppers. The babble of voices contained a mixture of languages—placid, sober Sumerian; complicated Hurrian; refined Akkadian. Although she could speak Hurrian, the language she needed with most merchants, she preferred her native tongue, Aramaic.

Now and then she stopped to inspect merchandise in the stalls. By the time she was ready to enter the wool merchant's shop, her basket held cinnamon, salt, and sprigs of fresh parsley.

"Welcome to my shop, Mistress Leah," the wool merchant Teshar said pleasantly. "Will you rest awhile here on my rug?"

"Thank you, Master Teshar. I'll just look at your lengths of cloth. I'm considering a new robe for my oldest son, and I haven't had time to weave it." Leah figured various pieces of woolen cloth.

"Your oldest son," Teshar remarked, "that's Reuben, isn't it?"

"Yes, Reuben."

"I understand Jacob has five sons already. That's a fine number.

"Five is a fine number," she agreed.

"As you know, my wife died after giving me only three daughters—no sons." He stepped closer, close enough so she could smell the sweet aromatic oil on his hair and beard. "I was wrong years ago when I asked for Rachel instead of for you. I should have asked for you. Together we could have produced sons. I put off going to your father again until it was too late."

Leah experienced the old flush of embarrassment that she used to feel when Teshar complemented her. It rose from somewhere beneath her robe and colored her face with its warmth. Before she could think of a reply, he went on in his low voice. "Doesn't it get lonely in your tent at night?" He edged even closer, the sleeve of his robe brushing against her. "As an old friend, I could help overcome your loneliness. I know which is your tent. I could find my way there tonight."

Leah could feel the warmth of his closeness. With frightening insight she knew she liked his attention. No other man had ever made her think that she was desirable. She was frightened not only by his invitation but by her reaction to it.

Abruptly she backed away from him. He followed, this time facing her. "You would like to have me come, wouldn't you?"

Suddenly Leah wanted to lean against him, to put her head on his shoulder. She realized how desperately lonely she really was. "No," she whispered. "No, you mustn't." She took a step backward.

"The goddess of love would be happy to have us love each other," Teshar suggested.

"The goddess of love? She's only a bronze figure."

"She wouldn't like to hear you talk that way."

"She has no power over me," Leah answered calmly. "I worship only the Lord."

"You've gotten this crazy idea from Jacob. You know your husband is an outsider. What kind of woman are you that you would stop worshiping your father's gods?"

Silently she turned away from him to the bolts of cloth piled on a rug.

Teshar sighed. "I see your mind is made up. As my gift to you, choose any piece of cloth you want for your son's robe."

Leah bit her lower lip. Absentmindedly she rubbed the cloth. "Thank you," she replied, choking out the words. "I can't decide today. I'll come back another time." Afraid to look at him, she walked out of his shop without glancing back.

Later that afternoon Leah stood by her cooking fire, patting out flatbread. She was still shaken by the conversation with Teshar and the realization of the feelings that she still had for him.

Reuben scurried around the side of the tent and ran to her. "Mama! Guess what I found out in the wheat fields?" He held his hands behind his back.

"The wheat fields! I've told you never to go into them. You know how dangerous that is, especially at harvesttime. The farmers could attack you with their harvesting knives."

"I didn't go into the wheat fields. I just found something along the edge."

"That's too close, Reuben."

"But wait till you see what I brought."

"All right. What did you bring?"

"Mandrakes!" With a flourish he whisked the plants from behind his back and held them up to her. "See. They have ripe fruit on them. One of Grandfather's shepherds helped me pull them up by the roots. Take them, Mama. They're for you."

"They're for me?" She accepted the plants. "Thank you, Reuben." What did this boy know about mandrakes?

Reuben shifted from one bare foot to the other. "Uh— Mama, the shepherds told me that if a woman eats some mandrake she'll make a baby. I heard you tell Aunt Rachel you wanted a baby, so I guess you'll want to eat some."

I know a better way to conceive, she thought. *Lie with your husband at the right time of the moon.* "You're a good boy, Reuben. Thank you for taking care of your mother."

"The bread dough smells good. Can I have a piece?"

She pinched off a generous piece and handed it to the boy.

He went into the tent, leaving her to contemplate the mandrakes in her hands.

They gave off a strong odor, rank and unpleasant—yet somehow compelling. Her mother used to emphasize the importance of mandrakes. She had said a woman might eat the fruit, but if she wanted to conceive a male child, she should soak the bark of the mandrake rout in wine and then sip some of the wine each day. Now at harvesttime when the fruit turned yellow, the roots were the most potent.

Rachel drifted over from her tent. Her attention riveted on the mandrake plants—the round yellow fruit, the broad wavy green leaves, the forked roots that resembled a human torso with long thin legs and slender arms.

"Where did Reuben find them?"

"At the edge of the wheat field," her sister answered absentmindedly.

"Please, Leah," Rachel suddenly begged, "give me some of the mandrakes."

Leah felt her anger rising. How could she have more babies when Rachel insisted that their husband spend his nights in her tent? The pent-up feelings exploded. "You've taken away my husband. Would you take away my son's mandrakes also?"

Rachel's gaze never left the brown roots of the plants. "You're my sister. Sisters are supposed to share. Why won't you give me some of them?"

"Sisters are supposed to share? Why won't you share Jacob with me?"

"Jacob chooses where he spends his nights. Can I help it if he spends them in my tent?"

"Can I help it if my son chooses to bring mandrakes to me?"

"I need him," Rachel said slowly. "If I don't give birth to a child, I think—I think I'll die."

Leah winced at the thought—Rachel, the child she had raised as if she were her own daughter. "Truly, Rachel, I don't wish the curse of barrenness on you. But Reuben brought the mandrakes for me, and I want another child. How can I have more children if Jacob never comes to my tent?"

She hesitated only a moment. "If you will give me the plants, I'll let you have him tonight."

Silently Leah handed the mandrakes to her sister. Rachel hurried back to her tent.

"Reuben, where are you?"

He came out of the tent. "Here, Mama."

"Watch for your father. Tell me when you see him coming from the fields. I want to meet him before he reaches the camp."

The sun was setting over the wheat field, giving it a golden glow. The stalks waved in the evening breeze. When she neared Jacob, Leah noticed that his shoulders sagged. He was tired after the many hours of watching her father's flocks. The extra strain of wheat harvest time and the animosity of the farmers took their toll every year.

"Do you wish to rest a few minutes?" she asked. He sat down and stretched out his legs.

"I have a sturdy tent with soft sheepskins," she added.

Jacob glanced at her. "Why are you telling me this?"

"My tent is a good place to rest after a day in the fields."

He looked at her doubtfully. "Are you so bold that you are asking me to spend the night with you?"

"You must come into my tent, because I have hired you with Reuben's mandrakes."

"What do you mean, you've hired me with Reuben's mandrakes?"

"Reuben brought some mandrake plants to me. Rachel and I made a bargain. For her—the mandrake plants. For me—a night with you."

"You mean that you and Rachel bargained for me?" His beard jutted out in front of him as he threw back his head and shook with laughter. "Women!" he exclaimed. "I'm too tired to understand you women." Rising, he headed toward the camp.

Leah followed, powerfully aware of his broad back, his strong shoulders, the proud lift of his head. She smiled. The time of the moon was right. Perhaps this very night Jacob would plant new seed for her next child.

Chapter 13

The joy of embracing Jacob again matched the happiness Leah felt a month later when she knew she was expecting a child. She hadn't needed those mandrakes.

Leaving her cooking fire, she lifted the tent flap. After a night in the pasture Jacob had come to her early this morning. Now he lay sprawled in deep sleep on the sheepskins. The morning light though the opening highlighted the gray that was becoming evident in his dark-brown hair and beard.

Their sons still slept also—Reuben on his stomach, Simeon and Levi together, Judah stirring in the first bit of wakefulness.

Jacob yawned and opened his eyes. "Leah," he called softly, "come here."

She knelt beside him.

"Tell me, are you carrying the seed I planted?"

Hesitantly she answered. She was reluctant to let him know so soon. He would no longer need to come to her if she was pregnant, but he had asked and she must tell. "Yes, I'm carrying your seed."

She looked at the four little boys in the tent. How many more of Jacob's sons would she bring into the world?

Less than two years later her tent held six sons. The new babies Issachar and Zebulun slept near their brothers Simeon, Levi, and Judah. Reuben was now old enough to spend the night in his father's tent. In Zilpah's tent the maid cared for Gad and Asher, the sons she had brought into the world for Leah.

Out in the pasture Laban congratulated Jacob. "Ten sons! Six with Leah, two with Zilpah, and two with Bilhah. You have done well."

"Yes, I've done well. I realize also that I have a big

responsibility," he added in a tired voice.

"How many sons do you want?"

"Twelve will be enough. If the Lord blesses me with two more, I will praise His name forever." He looked toward Rachel's tent. "If only Rachel could carry them. My hopes and my prayers are that she will produce two sons."

A few weeks later Leah took a jug and a leather bucket to the well for water. When she heard footsteps behind her, she turned in surprise to find Zilpah running after her.

"Mistress Leah," the servant woman said breathlessly.

"What's happened? Why are you following me?"

"Mistress, please may I discuss something with you?"

"You may, but what is so important that you must talk about it right now?"

Zilpah took the water jug. "I've been thinking about asking you something and suddenly decided I didn't want to wait another minute."

Leah stared at her for a moment. "What do you want to ask me?"

"Master Jacob no longer comes to my tent. He says two sons by me are enough. And he told Bilhah the same thing. Please, Mistress Leah, I've missed my friendship with you. Please, Mistress, could you ask Master Jacob to give me back to you?"

They had reached the well. Using a rope tied to its handle, Leah let the leather bucket down into the water. She pulled it up and poured the cool water into the jug. "Consider yourself mine again. I'll speak to Jacob and let him know."

They embraced each other.

"I have a secret I can tell you right now," Leah confided a few minutes later. "Jacob no longer comes to me. He goes only to Rachel because he wants her to bear two sons that will enlarge his number to 12, but here is my secret. Before he stopped, I was already carrying his next child."

"What will Rachel say when she finds out?"

"I don't know." Conflicting emotions crossed her face, and she struggled for words. "I'm worried about her. She looks frail. Poor Rachel. Barrenness is a terrible curse."

A few days later Rachel stood at the entrance to Leah's tent. Leah looked up in surprise. Her sister seldom came to her tent. "Come in, Rachel. Here, sit on this cushion."

Rachel eyed the cushion and then lowered herself slowly onto it. For a few moments she twisted one of the cushion's tassels between her fingers. Finally she gave a slight cough and asked, "Do you remember when I was a little girl, how I always came to you if I had a problem or if I had something happy to share?"

"I remember," Leah said softly, thinking back to the years after their mother died. "I liked it when you brought me your problems and your happy times. I remember holding you on my lap while you cried the morning Mother died. It was like you were my own little girl. I thought I was much older because you were so young."

"I remember that too," Rachel said wistfully. She lapsed into silence. Leah waited for her to speak again, waited for whatever had brought her in such a quiet mood. Rachel at the moment was not the rival wife, but the lonely little sister.

"You know how unhappy I've been because I've never had a child," Rachel finally said.

"I know," Leah answered sympathetically.

"You have children, so maybe it's hard for you to really understand how I feel."

"I've tried to understand. What is a woman without children?"

Rachel shifted on the cushion and curled a strand of her long dark hair around her finger. "Now I need to ask you a question. Do you remember Father's household goddess of love?"

The question surprised Leah. She hadn't thought of the deity for a long time. "Of course I remember her."

Rachel gazed across the tent, her fingers picked at the hem of her robe. Leah waited patiently until her sister continued. "Do you think it's safe to ask the goddess for help?"

Leah's thoughts reverted to her mother again and to how her mother had begged the love goddess for a son. How tragic the birth of that son turned out! The baby was stillborn, and her mother had died.

"I never ask the goddess of love for help," Leah finally replied. "Jacob says she's just a piece of bronze." Then she added firmly, "The love goddess has no power. You must ask the Lord for help."

Taking a deep breath, Rachel shut her eyes tightly. Tears glistened below her eyelids. "Sometimes I ask the Lord for help, but I want to be sure to ask the right god or goddess for safe delivery because—because I'm going to have a baby."

Leah dropped down onto a cushion opposite Rachel. She stared at her sister, the one their husband Jacob loved most. Leah had tried to gain his love by giving him children. It had not worked. He had still loved Rachel more. Now with Rachel having a child, his dreams with her would be fulfilled. Leah did not want her sister to continue to bear the curse of barrenness—no, especially not Rachel—but . . . Now she could do nothing to compete against her—her rival, her sister—the sister she loved so much. "You're going to have a baby? That . . . that's wonderful," she stammered softly.

Rachel opened her eyes and held her hands to her mouth. "But I'm afraid. I'm so afraid that something might go wrong."

Leah reached over to touch her sister's arm. "I'm sure nothing will go wrong, and I'm so happy for you."

"Are you really?"

The words were hard to say, but she did mean them. "Yes I am. I wouldn't wish otherwise for any woman."

"Even the woman your husband loves?"

Leah said nothing.

"Jacob loves me, but you have eight sons already. I can claim only two sons because Bilhah had them for me. Now at last I'm carrying a child, but I could never catch up with you. I wonder which is more important—Jacob's love or children."

Rachel covered her face with her hands. Her voice sounded smothered. "You're ahead of me, Leah. You're Jacob's first wife, and this would never have happened if I hadn't flirted with Teshar."

Leah frowned. What was troubling her sister that she would bring up the old struggle they had gone through over the merchant's affection? "That was years ago. What in the world does this have to do with Teshar?"

"If I hadn't flirted with him, he would have asked Father for you instead of for me. Then I would have been Jacob's first wife." She wiped tears away with her hand.

Leah's mind raced back to the hurt she had felt when Teshar had asked for her sister. Now she was glad that Rachel had flirted with the wool merchant. If she hadn't, Leah would never have been Jacob's wife at all. "Let's think about your baby," she said, trying to change the subject. "You'll feel better when the baby begins to move."

Rachel gave no indication that she had heard. She sat with

her head down, and her voice was so low Leah could barely make out her words. "If something happens to me, will you take care of my baby?"

Leah knelt beside her and encircled her thin shoulders with her arm. Rachel was the younger sister who needed a mother once more. "Of course. You're my sister. We're family. Father always taught us to take care of family."

Rachel wiped her eyes again. "You have all those sons for Jacob to love. If I have only one, I want Jacob to love my son as much as all yours put together. He will love mine best of all. He will. I know he will. I know it."

She pulled away from Leah's arm and slipped out of the tent, leaving her sister alone with her thoughts.

How would Rachel's child change Jacob's love for his other children? Leah pictured the scene she had observed so many times. As soon as one of her boys started to walk, Jacob encouraged the child to toddle after him to the pasture. From that early age he prepared his sons to love the work of a shepherd.

Often he carried the child back to her on his shoulders and left him in her arms. Now that the boys were older, Jacob was teaching them to watch over the animals and to help hold them while he sheared.

Leah felt a sudden chill. "Lord of heaven," she prayed, "let my sons continue to have their father's love."

Several months later the trek up to Haran from winter pasture seemed longer than usual. Leah glanced back at her sister. Rachel lagged behind the other women and children as they plodded along the rocky ground.

"Reuben," Leah called to her oldest son, "take care of the little boys riding on the donkeys. I'm going to wait for your aunt Rachel."

Leah shifted Dinah, her newest infant, from her left arm to her right, readjusting the long shawl firmly around herself and her child.

"Rachel," she said when her sister caught up. "Let's sit and rest awhile."

Supporting her full abdomen, Rachel sank slowly onto a ledge of rock by the side of the trail. "I'm so heavy," she complained.

Worry gripped Leah. Her sister's slender arms and legs had

105

thinned even more during her pregnancy. The child was due any day now. Fortunately they would reach Haran before the expected time of birth. Even robust women found it hard to give birth and then travel on with the caravan—and Rachel was far from robust.

The sisters sat together quietly. *She needs rest,* thought Leah, *and so do I.*

The entire migration had exhausted her. The weather turned unseasonably warm the second day. The flocks, restless and unruly, kept the shepherds busy rounding up the strays. Levi cut his hand on a sharp rock and Simeon hit a shepherd's child, giving the little boy a bruised eye. Jacob's quiet nature gave way to an occasional burst of temper as he carried the responsibility of bringing Laban's flocks safely to Haran.

"We're almost there," Leah said. "We'll reach home pastureland before dark."

"I hope so. It's so hard to walk."

Once again Leah found herself the battleground of conflicting emotions. It was good to share with Rachel the joy of her sister's impending childbirth. The pleasure of two women sharing the experience of pregnancy and motherhood. Rachel had been denied that for many years. But another emotion fought for dominance—fear that Rachel would have a male child, a son for Jacob, and that he would give all his love to her son. Leah had never forgotten her sister's words, "He will love my son best of all."

In her lap Dinah wiggled as best she could in her swaddling clothes. She opened her eyes—those clear, dark eyes that her mother loved. Leah held the infant to her lips and kissed the smooth forehead, enjoying the warm, baby smell of her daughter.

Simeon and Levi shuffled along the way, kicking at clods of dirt. "Mama," Simeon shouted, "can I carry Dinah for a while?"

She placed the child against his chest and wrapped her shawl securely around both the baby and Simeon to keep Dinah from falling. "Don't go too far from me," she warned. "I need to feed her soon."

"Look here, Levi," Simeon said to his younger brother. "This is a girl."

The smaller boy stared at him. "I know she's a girl."

"Don't ever forget it," Simeon went on in a serious voice.

"She's the only girl we've got. We have to take good care of her."

Levi's shrill voice matched his. "I'll never let anything bad happen to our sister. She's the only one we've got."

"Hush," Leah soothed the excited boys. "No one is going to hurt Dinah. Let's go now. It's still a long walk to Haran. Levi, help your aunt Rachel to stand up."

In the home pastureland outside Haran's walls, Laban and his oldest son Kesad waited for the caravan. Two shepherd boys had arrived the day before to inform him that Jacob was bringing the flocks up from winter pasture. Four months had passed since Laban had examined the flocks, four months since he had seen his daughters and his grandsons.

Leah had gone south with a full belly. Did he have a new grandson? Rachel too might arrive with her first child in her arms.

In the distance the sound of bleating heralded the approach of the caravan—sheep and goats, daughters and grandsons, Laban's possessions and wealth.

Now he could make out figures among the first flock. Jacob strode at the head, leading the way.

"Father," Kesad asked, "why do you let Jacob take more than half of your animals without supervision? I could have gone to keep an eye on him."

"I'm not so young anymore," Laban replied. "I need you with me."

"I know we can't pasture all the flocks in one place, but you have my brothers to help you."

"I trust Jacob," his father said in a low voice.

"I don't! He could sell sheep along the way and we would never know." Kesad's voice squeaked slightly as it change from deep to high, the voice of a boy who was fast becoming a man.

The lad was right, of course. Laban didn't really trust Jacob. He knew he had a hold over his son-in-law—the bride-price, seven years of labor for Leah, seven for Rachel.

Shearing time was fast approaching. Fourteen years Jacob had worked. He would complete payment of the bride-price at shearing time, and the secure hold Laban had enjoyed would vanish.

The caravan started to enter the pastureland. With satisfaction Laban gazed at the first large flock. The sheep moved in ripples—each individual animal pushing, shoving the others along, keeping the momentum going.

The shepherds now scattered them over the pasture. The eager animals hurried into the grassland and immediately wanted to graze. Jacob and his men urged them ahead to make room for the rest of the flocks.

Laban spotted a blur of motion. Simeon raced across the field with Levi close behind. Reaching his grandfather first, Simeon jumped up and down in front of Laban. "Grandfather, we've got a girl," he shouted.

Levi panted to a stop next to Simeon. "It's a girl," he repeated.

"Mama is holding her now, but sometimes I get to carry her," Simeon exclaimed.

"A girl?" Laban questioned.

The women began unloading tents from the donkeys. Laban looked past the pack animals to the last figures—Leah and Rachel, his daughters, each carrying a baby, Leah's in her arms, Rachel's still in her belly. The younger daughter limped along slowly.

Leah remained by her sister's side although she wanted to dash ahead to greet her father. Laban came to meet them. He kissed the two women on their cheeks and the baby on the forehead.

"Welcome home, daughters."

Rachel groaned and sank to her knees on the ground. She folded her hands under her stomach. "I'm so tired."

"Zilpah," Leah called, "help Bilhah put up Rachel's tent."

Through the night Rachel labored in great agony. Her thin body refused to give up the child. Leah stayed with her, wiping her hot face, offering words of encouragement. Bilhah prepared the birthing stones, and Zilpah examined Rachel frequently for signs of delivery.

The sun was already high the next morning when the servant woman pulled the child into the world. "You have a son," she announced.

Rachel was too weak to whisper more than one word, a name for the newborn. "Joseph."

"Thanks and praise to the Lord," Leah breathed, "the baby is finally here."

She felt exhausted, drained of energy, flooded with relief that her sister would recover, yet a disturbing thought nagged at her. A son for Jacob. Surely now he would favor Rachel's child and pay less attention to hers.

Leah looked at Rachel pressing her cheek against her new son's head. The new mother's tired face was beautiful in its happiness. The words Rachel had spoken months before crowded into Leah's mind. "He will love my son best of all. He will. I know he will. I know it."

Chapter 14

A week later Leah sat nursing Dinah. From outside the tent Jacob's voice startled her. "Leah, are you in there?" He lifted the flap and entered.

Leah laid the child on a sheepskin and faced her husband. "What is it?"

He took her by the arm and pulled her outside. "Let me look at your eyes."

Instinctively she shut them tightly. "No one ever wants to look at my eyes."

"Please open your eyes. I want to see them."

"Why do you want to see my eyes?"

"They're going to help me breed the sheep and goats."

Her eyes opened in surprise. "Help you breed the sheep and goats? How?"

"During the last breeding season, I had a strange dream, a dream that could change my life. I'll tell you about it, but first I want to see your eyes. Since you're always squinting, I've never really looked into them." He gazed intently at her in the slanting afternoon light.

She wanted to cover them with her hands, to run back into the tent and hide her face against a sheepskin, but his intense gaze and his firm grip on her arm forced her to stay.

Cupping her face in his hands, he gently tilted her head until she had to look up at him. The warm pressure of his hands and his deep-set brown eyes held her immobile.

"Your eyes are light brown with flecks of gold," he said.

Pulling away from him, she lowered her head in embarrassment. "And they squint," she murmured.

"Did anyone else in your family have eyes like yours?"

"I remember my grandmother had weak eyes. She was my

110

mother's mother, and her eyes were light brown like mine."

"That's it!" Jacob gave a triumphant laugh. "That's it. I always thought that only males could pass on physical characteristics, but since my dream I've had some new thoughts. I don't know how, but some features could be transmitted through the female too."

Leah looked at him in wonder. "You mean that I got my weak eyes from my grandmother?"

"Exactly! But with the help of your father. In his family there must have been ancestors with eyes like yours too. They were bound to reappear."

"What does this have to do with the sheep and goats?"

Her husband smiled. "The Lord sent me a dream. In it I saw strong buck goats leaping upon the flocks. They were mating with the strongest doe goats. But this is the important part." He lowered his voice. "You must promise not to tell any of this to your father."

"I promise."

"The important part is that the goats were spotted. The Lord's message is clear."

"It's not clear to me."

"The Lord's message is for me to breed the liveliest males, both goats and sheep of course, with the females that are the strongest."

Leah shook her head in puzzlement.

"Because even though they look unspotted, both the males and the females carry the tendency to have spotted offspring. The marks might skip a generation or two, like the weak eyes skipped your mother, but then the spotted animals will reappear."

"I don't understand. Why is this important to you? Why do you want to breed for spotted animals? Are they better than white sheep and black goats?"

"No, they're not better, but I need flocks of my own. I'll bargain with your father for all the spotted animals as my wages. Although there aren't many of them now, the Lord has shown me how to breed the ones that don't show spots to produce an increasing number of spotted offspring."

He put his hand under Leah's chin and raised her head. His eyes searched hers again. "You have helped me, Leah. When I had that dream, I wondered what it meant. Then the Lord reminded me of your eyes. What you told me about your

111

grandmother shows how characteristics can pass from one generation to another." He let go of her chin and lifted his face to the sky. "Praise to the Lord. In a few years I'll have strong flocks of my own."

Leah stared at him in a confusion of happiness that she might have helped him and of unbelief that it was true. "Did my eyes really help you? Will you really have large flocks and your own shepherds to care for them?"

"Yes. I'll become rich and I'll have shepherds and sheep dogs to herd the flocks."

"Dogs! They're the enemies of sheep."

"Not the sheep dogs of Canaan. They're intelligent and they're trained to guard the sheep."

"Dogs kill baby lambs."

"Not sheep dogs. You'll see, you'll see." He left, swinging along in a confident stride toward the pasture.

Laban watched him approach. "Jacob has 11," he muttered to his son Kesad, "11 male children. The gods bless him in whatever he does. I suppose he'll want to return to his father in Canaan now that he has worked out the bride-price."

"Let him go. You have sons, too. We can take care of the flocks."

They stood at the edge of the pastureland. As Jacob walked toward them, Kesad edged away from his father.

"Peace," Laban greeted his nephew.

"Peace," Jacob answered.

Laban looked across the pasture. "I've been examining the flocks."

"Are you satisfied that the sheep and goats I brought up from winter pasture last week are healthy?" the younger man asked.

"I'm satisfied that they are healthy. You have cared well for the flocks."

"For 14 years," Jacob reminded him.

"For 14 years," Laban echoed, careful not to show that he understood the allusion.

"I'm saying that I've paid the bride-price for my wives."

"So you have, so you have."

Jacob had given the official announcement of payment. Laban knew he must answer with a legal sentence recognizing the fulfillment of obligation. Reluctantly he spoke. "You have completed the payment of your debt."

"I've paid, but I know that the law in Haran says that daughters and their children still belong to the father even after the husband has paid the bride-price."

Laban nodded in satisfaction. "That's true. They belong to me. You must provide for my daughters and my grandchildren, but they are my possessions just as much as all my flocks."

"The law also states that you could give me my wives and my sons. Let me have them. I've paid my debt to you and now I want to return to my own country."

Laban stroked his beard, then slid his hand over his mouth to hide a smile. He still had a hold over his son-in-law. Not only did Jacob have to ask for his wives and children, he would also have to request wages. He needed to save up sufficient resources for the long trip back to Canaan. If Laban were careful, that could take years, maybe even Jacob's entire lifetime.

"My two daughters have carried 11 sons for you," Laban shifted the conversation to his advantage, hoping to put Jacob in a position of begging.

"The Lord has blessed me. He has also blessed you wherever I work. Your flocks have increased. I've given you good service."

"True. My flocks have increased," Laban agreed with studied calmness. Carefully avoiding his son-in-law's request for Leah and Rachel, he offered, "Name your wages. What shall I give you?"

"You'll not give me anything." Jacob looked straight at him and his voice intensified. "I'll earn what I get."

"Name your wages," Laban repeated, concentrating on his kinsman's every word and tone of voice. Thoroughly aware that Jacob could manipulate a shrewd bargain, he knew he must remain alert to keep the upper hand.

"I will feed and tend your flocks again, in exchange for every spotted sheep and goat. I will work out the price over a period of time."

Now here was a bargain to Laban's liking. His flocks did contain some spotted animals, but most of the sheep were white and nearly all the goats were black. The main part of the flocks would still belong to him. He nodded. "Let it be as you have said. When do you want these animals?"

"Today. They will be my flock. When they produce, I will give the unspotted offspring to you, keeping only the spotted for myself. This way we will be able to tell our flocks apart."

"And you will tend my flocks in payment for these animals, even if it takes years?"

"Even if it takes years, as long as you understand that I will have all the future-born spotted animals from your large flocks also."

Laban considered his last request for a moment. Slowly he nodded. "We'll bargain again for the length of your service after I count the number of animals that you take now. Tell the shepherds to remove the spotted sheep and goats from the flocks. You shall have them today."

As Jacob hurried away to take care of the division, Kesad returned. Together he and Laban watched Jacob giving instructions to the shepherds.

"I heard him," Kesad said to his father. "He's not stupid. He's up to something."

Laban frowned and pulled at his beard. "You have a point there. He could be up to something. What do you think he's planning?"

Kesad answered uneasily, "After the animals are divided, he'll have a flock that's big enough to support a journey to Canaan. All he needs to do is trade sheep or goats for supplies along the way."

His father continued to tug at his beard. "He could easily pack up and leave during the night when I'm sleeping in Haran. The shepherds like him. He might even persuade some to go with him."

"Father, you can't let him get away with a scheme like that."

"I won't," Laban grunted. "If he thinks he can trick me, I'll outwit him first. He can have the spotted animals born in the future, but I'll not let him get a head start with these now." He rubbed his hands in agitation. "Get your brothers. We'll take all the spotted sheep and goats into the mountains." He glanced up at the afternoon sun. "We'll leave tonight."

Kesad ran across the field to find his brothers.

The sun was sinking below the pasture when Jacob took a seat on a rug by Leah's fire. Holding Dinah in one arm, she handed her husband a bowl of lentils flavored with thyme and coriander. He set it down in front of him. Standing up, he hit his clenched right fist into the palm of his left hand.

"Your father has deceived me again," he growled. "He

114

agreed to let me have a flock made up of all the spotted animals. I agreed to work out the payment over a period of time. But tonight he's taking all the sheep and goats that should be mine into the mountains."

His words sent a tremor through her. "That can't be. Why would Father do that? How do you know?"

"I have friends among the shepherds."

Leah shifted Dinah to her shoulder. "I thought shearing started tomorrow. I've never known Father to leave before shearing. Something's wrong. What is it?"

"By withholding the flock from me, your father is trying to keep me here, but I won't have to depend upon him forever. He's left the unspotted flocks in my care. I know how to breed them to produce some spotted offspring, and I'll make sure I get them and keep them. When I have flocks, I'll have my own shepherds and my dogs to guard them."

Jacob spit out the next words. "In spite of your father, I'll build my flocks. It'll take a while, a few years, but as soon as I do, we'll leave for Canaan."

"Canaan!" she exclaimed. "Canaan is so far away."

"It's my land," he stated flatly. "You'll have to learn to like it." Resuming his seat, he spooned the lentil soup into his mouth with pieces of flatbread. When the bowl was empty, he left it on the rug. "I'm going to see how my new son fared today."

As he headed toward Rachel's tent, Leah picked up the bowl and stared into it. She was unaware of Simeon until he pulled on her robe, interrupting her troubled thoughts.

"Why doesn't Father hold Dinah once in a while?" the little boy asked.

"Hush, Simeon," she said softly. She disliked any reminder of her own fear—the fear that Joseph would take Jacob's love away from her children. But her mind was too full of the struggle between him and her father to think of that now. How could her father hide the spotted sheep and goats that he had promised to her husband? How could her father break his word to his own kinsman? Of course he had done it before. Memories of his deception and her wedding night flooded back to her.

"Here," she said to Simeon, "you may hold Dinah while I put away the bowl."

The boy held out his arms to take the baby. "Joseph is only a week old," he muttered, "and already he's Father's favorite." He carried his little sister toward the tent.

115

Still holding the empty bowl, Leah sat down by the fire and stared into its flames.

That night she stirred restlessly on her bed. The sounds of sheep and goats being driven off into the darkness disrupted her sleep. Several times she got up to open the tent flap. Shivering from the chilly air, she peered into the night.

Sometime before dawn Dinah cried hungrily and Leah nursed her. The sky finally lightened. Leah rose in time to see Jacob leave his tent and head toward the pasture.

Later she prepared the midmorning meal to take to him. As she walked to the pasture, her feet felt as heavy as her heart. After the unusual disturbance during the night, the sheep were easily frightened. Bleating in alarm, they darted away from her. The goats too were skittish.

Jacob stood by an acacia bush, gazing out over the flock of white sheep and black goats. She handed him flatbread and a pot of hot, mashed garbanzo beans. "I'll start shearing tomorrow," he remarked quietly.

"How can you be so calm after what my father did to you?"

"Don't forget what I learned from my dream and from your eyes," he reminded her, "about breeding the strongest animals because they carry the tendencies for spots. By this time next year I'll have my first flock." He turned from the pasture to stare down at her. "When your father comes back from the mountains, I'll not give him the satisfaction of an argument."

Leah detected seething anger beneath his low, evenly spaced words.

Jacob had the shearing well under way before his father-in-law returned from the mountains. "I left Kesad and Jabal to oversee the flock and the shepherds," Laban announced, then turned his attention to the merchants who arrived every day to buy wool and goat hair.

At the end of shearing season, without a confrontation but in hostile silence, Laban and Jacob readied the caravan to head north.

Leah moved in a daze as she prepared for the journey to summer pasture. Year after year she had taken down her tent, folded it, and put it on a donkey. Year after year she had followed her father and her husband north. How many more times would she go north before she must travel south instead, follow Jacob to Canaan, never to return to Haran?

Together Laban and Jacob led the caravan into the mountains. There Laban left his son-in-law in charge of the flocks while he continued another day's journey into a side valley to check on his sons and the spotted animals with them.

With effort Leah raised her tent. Weariness from the journey and from the tension between her father and her husband threatened to engulf her. After she had it erect, she sat outside to rest before preparing the evening meal. Her gaze went to the high peaks—those northern mountains that she loved.

She thought of what it might be like to travel south to Canaan. She had heard that the land around Beersheba was harsh and bare, a dry wilderness of low, rolling hills. Travelers told of a lifeless salt sea, of a valley where the earth trembled frequently. With a shake of her head she thrust the thought aside and got up to build her cooking fire.

By the next shearing season, through clever breeding of the strongest animals, Jacob owned a young flock of spotted sheep and goats, all healthy and lively. He hired shepherds. A year later after shearing and selling the wool and goat hair, he bought donkeys and his first pair of camels.

It was the following year, while he was shearing in the pastureland near Haran, that a line of camels headed toward his camp.

Zilpah stood up from the cooking fire and shielded her eyes against the sun low in the western sky. "Look, a caravan is coming this way from the south," she reported to Leah. "Master Jacob has seen it too. He's walking up from the pasture, and Reuben is with him."

"Jacob is waiting for the dogs," Leah replied. "Every caravan that arrives from the south, he hopes it's the one bringing the sheep dogs that he ordered. I don't know why he wants them." She watched the caravan as it advanced steadily toward the camp. "I'd be happy if he never got the dogs, but that caravan is headed this way for some reason."

The drivers halted the camels near Leah's tent. The caravan leader stepped forward. Behind him two dogs eyed the encampment. The leader shouted at them, and they circled him warily and then stood, alert and watchful, a short distance away.

Leah observed the dogs suspiciously. They were about the same height as a sheep. The heavily built male was white with large black spots. Black hair like a mask covered his eyes and

117

extended up to the tips of his ears, contrasting with the white of his throat.

The female was smaller. She was reddish-brown except for her white chest and feet.

Rachel hurried over from her tent with Joseph running along beside her. She stopped behind Leah and stared at the strangers.

"It looks like Jacob's dogs are here," Leah told her.

Jacob and Reuben approached the caravan leader, Jacob scrutinizing the waiting dogs. "You have brought them."

"All the way from the Negev Desert," the merchant replied. He nodded to a camel driver. "Bring the basket." Then with a wry smile he said to Jacob, "A week ago the female added five puppies to our load."

The driver removed a carrying basket from the side of a camel and brought it to the leader. Five puppies—three black-and-white, two brown—wiggled in the bottom.

"I had to contend with seven dogs instead of two during the last week. Two was bad enough. I expect good payment for these seven."

"How do I know the two are trained sheep dogs?" Jacob demanded. "How do I know that you have treated them well and that they are in good health?"

"See for yourself. There they are. Healthy and ready to go to work for you."

"Come," Jacob called to the dogs. Instantly their ears perked up. They recognized the command in his voice. Avoiding the caravan leader they ran to Jacob, their tails curved over their backs and wagging enthusiastically.

Jacob knelt and rubbed them behind their ears. After slowly and expertly examining the male and then the female with his hands, he stood. "We agreed on the price before you went to Canaan."

"I expect extra for the puppies." The trader picked one up and held it high for everyone to see.

"Extra for the puppies," Jacob agreed.

Leah shook her head in amazement—Jacob had agreed to the man's demand. He knelt again by the dogs, talking to them, scratching above their tails, letting them lick his face.

"Leah," he called to her. "Bring one of your baskets for the puppies."

Reluctantly she brought a basket from her tent. While Jacob handed over silver for the caravan leader to weigh out the agreed amount, Leah gingerly reached for the puppies and transferred them to her basket. She held the last one in her hands. It nuzzled against her searching for milk. Its soft nose and mouth pushed and rubbed. Cuddling the puppy against her shoulder, she smoothed the hair on its back. "You're just like any baby, aren't you?"

She glanced at the mother dog. Its eyes, brown and almond-shaped, watched anxiously. Leah smiled at Zilpah. "I might learn to like these animals as much as Jacob does."

Taking the puppy from her, Jacob stooped down and held it toward Joseph. "Look here, son. When this puppy is old enough to leave its mother, I'll give it to you for your very own. I'll train it to work of course, but when it's not working, it can sleep with you."

The boy reached to touch the puppy. Jacob smiled fondly and guided Joseph's hand onto the animal's back.

Leah looked away from Joseph, and her gaze rested on her son Reuben. He took a step closer to his father and held out his hands. Jacob kept his attention on Joseph, rubbing the little boy's hand along the puppy's back.

Resentment burned in her breast. Couldn't Reuben, her firstborn son, have a puppy, too? Could only Rachel's firstborn receive favors from Jacob?

"Here." Jacob handed the puppy to Leah. "Find a sheepskin for the mother to sleep on. Keep her and the puppies in your tent." He reached down and scratched the male dog along its back. "I'll take this one to pasture and put him to work right away."

Reuben looked at the dogs once more and then turned toward the pasture. "Here comes Grandfather."

When Laban had noticed the caravan stopped at the camp, he hurried up from the far pasture. Now he glanced from the caravan leader to Jacob. "What's all this? What are these dogs doing here?"

"I asked the caravan leader to bring them from Canaan," his son-in-law answered.

"You ordered these dogs brought here?" Laban snorted in disgust. "I want no murdering dogs in my pastureland."

"They're sheep dogs, trained to guard the flocks," Jacob replied. "Down," he ordered the dogs, and they lay down obediently at his feet, eyes open and alert.

"You know I disapprove of dogs. You've done this against my wishes."

Jacob faced the older man squarely. "I've done this because I know they'll work hard for me. They'll work loyally and without question. I can trust them."

Laban's jaw ground from side to side. "Just keep them away from my flocks," he growled.

Leah still held the puppy. It whimpered. She edged away from her father, sheltering the little dog from his sight. She cuddled it against her breast to comfort it and to quiet the agitation in her own heart. The breach between her father and her husband was steadily deepening. How long had it been since she had seen them sit together after the evening meal to discuss the day's work?

It had been too long. Too long.

Chapter 15

Leah bought fine white goat wool, imported from a northern land, from the wool merchant. She wove it into a new robe for Dinah's sixth birthday.

A few days later Jacob drew his wives together. "The Lord has told me that I must leave Haran and return to Canaan."

Leah had always known that a time would come when Jacob would say, "We'll leave for Canaan." Now that dreaded occasion had arrived. She and Rachel were his wives and they must go where their husband led them.

"When?" Rachel asked.

"Your father left this morning to shear the sheep that he keeps in the mountains. We'll leave while he's gone."

"We can't go without saying goodbye to Father."

"Yes, we can," Jacob told her, although there was compassion in his voice. "You know your father could prevent us from leaving."

"Yes," Rachel agreed softly. "We can't say goodbye to Father. After all, we're his possessions. He owns us."

"Start packing," Jacob ordered. "Be ready tomorrow. We need to leave right away before the Euphrates River rises from the melting snow in the mountains and while there is still spring grass for the animals along the way." He walked back to the pasture.

"Beersheba in Canaan is Jacob's home," Leah said, "but Haran is ours. I love it here. How can we like that foreign place?"

"We'll have to learn to like it," her sister replied.

With a heavy heart Leah led the way back to the tents. "Everything there will be different. We'll even have to learn a strange Canaanite language to use in the marketplace."

Early the next morning she knelt on a rug in her father's house. What should she take along to Canaan? Clothing and keepsakes lay on the rug in front of her: her wedding robe, the embroidery still unspoiled; her bridal sheet, the linen had turned yellow; the musk perfume jar, now empty with a lingering sweet scent; Reuben's tunic, the first article of clothing she had woven for any of her children. He had worn it when he was learning to walk.

"Hurry," Rachel warned. "We have to leave before Ahera wakes up." She shifted the goatskin bag slung over her shoulder.

"I'm having a hard time deciding what to take with me."

"Just put what you want in your bag and come on."

"Yes, I know I should hurry." Leah folded the wedding robe and put it in her bag. She stuffed in the bridal sheet. Dinah would need it someday. The tunic went next. She left the perfume jar standing on the rug.

Quickly Rachel picked up the remaining items, dumped them into a large basket, and pushed it into a corner of the room. She glanced outside the door to make sure no one would see them leave. "Let's go."

"I guess I'm ready."

The only person in the courtyard was Gamesh. He had opened the gate for them when they arrived, and now he dozed as his grandfather used to do, his back against the outside wall.

Leah stopped for a last look at the cooking stove where her mother had taught her to bake flatbread. She glanced at the old fig tree in the corner and at the oleander bushes growing along the courtyard wall. For a second she gazed at the door to the room where she had listened to the wedding feasts and waited for Jacob—the room where she had conceived Reuben.

"We'll never see Father's house again," she said sadly.

"You're right. We won't see it again." Rachel paused. "I'm sorry to leave, too, but we can't stop now. Come on, Leah. Think of the new land that we'll call home. Jacob says that Canaan is a good country with wide valleys for pasture."

They shut the gate behind them and headed for the road that would lead them to the fields.

"What did you take in your bag?" Leah asked.

"I just brought along a few keepsakes."

"It looks heavy."

"I hope Bilhah has packed my tent," Rachel changed the subject.

As they entered the camp, Leah was pleased to see that her tent was folded. Zilpah had prepared it for packing on a donkey.

Reuben rummaged in a basket. Simeon and Levi hovered over him.

"What are you boys doing here?" Leah asked. "Why aren't you helping your father?"

"We're hungry," Reuben answered. "We just came for some bread."

"You're looking in the wrong basket. Here, I'll find some for you." Leah opened a basket and handed rounds of flatbread to Simeon and Levi. They immediately started to munch on it. She gave a handful to Reuben. "Take some for the other boys."

"I'll take a piece to Father, too," Reuben said.

Levi started to walk toward the pasture and then turned back to stand in front of his mother. "On our way to Canaan, how are we going to get across the big river?"

"I can swim," Simeon announced.

"You can't swim across the river," Reuben warned. "Father says the Euphrates is wide and deep. We'll cross in a boat. They have boats along the caravan route."

"Mama," Levi sounded worried, "won't the boats sink when the camels get on them? I don't know how to swim."

Before Leah could think of an answer to calm him, Simeon shouted, "Look! Here comes Father's pet."

Joseph strolled over from Rachel's tent. "Aunt Leah, may I have some bread too."

She passed him a round of flatbread.

"How come you're not working like the rest of us?" Levi demanded.

"I'm only 6 years old," his half-brother answered.

Levi thrust out his lower lip. "I worked when I was 6."

"Father says I might get hurt around the sheep and goats."

"What about us?" Simeon yelled.

"Boys! Go back to work." Leah waved her hands toward the fields.

"We're going," Reuben sputtered. "Come on, Simeon and Levi. Leave the pet here with the women."

Leah sat down on the folded tent and held her head in her hands. Of course Joseph was Jacob's favorite. He had been ever since the moment of his birth. After all, he was Rachel's son.

When problems confronted her, Leah could usually work out a plan of action. At that moment, however, they overwhelmed her. Why did Jacob need her at all? He had 11 sons. The maidservants could cook and care for them. Rachel could give him love.

"Lord, help me," she prayed. "I feel useless."

And now to leave Haran, no longer to visit in her father's house, no longer to feel the security of having him near or waiting for them when they returned from pasture.

After they left Haran, what dangers lay ahead for her children? How would they safely cross the Euphrates River? She had never stepped onto a boat. Perhaps Levi was right. It might sink with a load of heavy camels. She couldn't swim, either. The children might fall into the river, and she knew of no way to save them from drowning.

If they did safely pass the river, what then? First—the desert where wolves and jackals roamed the hills and valleys. They followed the flocks, seizing lambs and kid goats and sometimes a small child.

Strange tribes of people lived in Canaan. She had heard harrowing tales of robbers. Bands of them swooped down on caravans, killing the men and capturing the women and children to sell as slaves.

And if that weren't enough, Jacob had told her he expected trouble from his brother Esau. Twenty years ago Esau had threatened to kill him.

Why had she agreed to go to Canaan? Of course she knew the answer. Love for Jacob. Although she had never told him, her love for her husband overruled all other thoughts and desires.

Her love for Jacob was so strong she had agreed to go while her father sheared his sheep three days' journey to the north—but she loved her father, too, and now she had no chance to say goodbye to him. She longed to kiss him one last time and thank him for giving her pretty clothes and jewelry when she was growing up.

True—he had used up her inheritance, the money he should have saved from the bride price, and he had deceived Jacob many times.

Still—he was her father, the head of the family. He had taught her the importance of tradition. Although she was a woman, she held distinction as his firstborn. She would remember his teachings.

It was too late to thank him. She couldn't trust her father completely, anyway. If he wished, he could claim her and Rachel and all of their children as his property since they were their father's possessions. They must leave without his knowledge.

She dropped her hands away from her face and realized they were wet with her tears. If only she didn't feel so useless. Who needed an aging, weak-eyed woman?

She felt a little arm around her neck and a face pressed against her wet one—Dinah's cheek against hers.

Leah had provided many sons for Jacob. Dinah was for her.

"Are you crying, Mama?"

"Yes."

"Why?"

"I guess it's hard to leave the place I've always lived."

"I think it's fun to ride on the camels." The child's eagerness lifted her spirits a bit.

"Leah!" She left Dinah and hurried to meet her husband.

"What is it?"

"I need your help. One of the camels refuses to get up. The driver found a nasty sore on its leg. Bring your herbs and see what you can do."

She dashed back for her herb basket. When the camel saw her, it curled its lips and bared its big, blunt teeth. Jacob and the camel driver poked at its head from either side to restrain it from biting her while she examined the leg.

"It looks like a fresh wound, a scrape of some type," she said. "It's not infected. I'll use comfrey."

From the basket she took a pottery bowl and filled it half full from her container of rendered tallow. Rubbing dried comfrey leaves between her fingers, she let the herb fragments drop into the bowl. Then she mixed the finely powdered leaves into the tallow until it took on the dark-green color of the comfrey.

"Watch the camel carefully," she instructed the two men. "I'm ready to apply the salve." She had no desire for the nervous animal to lash around and bite her.

When she touched its wound, the camel whined and tried to spit at her. Leah smeared on the salve and leaped away. With a word of command from the driver, the beast rocked to its feet, all the time protesting with spits and snorts. It towered on its long, lean legs and glared at her.

She hurried off to finish her packing.

"I need your help," Jacob had said when he called her to give aid to the camel. She felt more useful than she had a few minutes earlier, yet in tending the camel she had hastened the time to leave.

All her fears surfaced. Was there no turning back? Was there no possibility at least of delaying their move to an unknown land?

The driver led the camel toward her folded tent and her baskets.

Leah returned to Jacob. "Couldn't we wait until Father comes back so I can say goodbye to him?" she begged. Her eyes blurred with tears.

"He'll stop us from going."

"That's all right with me," she blurted in panic. "I don't want to go. I want to stay here near Haran. I want to stay near my father."

"Finish packing. We're going to Canaan. And we're leaving right now."

Three days later the Euphrates River was a streak of brightness across the plain. Reflected sunlight danced above the water. A cool west wind blew against the camels and their riders.

Leah shivered.

Perched behind her on the camel, Dinah clung to the back of Leah's robe. "We're almost to the river, Mama. I can see the big boat."

"That's good," her mother said without enthusiasm. After they ferried over the river, her home would lie behind her forever. The river would separate her from the land she loved and from her father.

Reuben rode alongside with Judah sitting behind him. Reuben whipped their camel to a run, its bells jangling wildly. Simeon and Levi, also riding together, raced after them, trying to reach the river first. The rest of the caravan straggled along behind. It was Jacob's wealth, his possessions—cattle, sheep, goats, donkeys, camels, shepherds, servants, and dogs.

To avoid the marshy ground where the Balikh River emptied into the broad Euphrates, Jacob circled to the right. At last they rode onto dry, stony ground at the river's edge.

Leah's heart jumped when first she saw the ferry—a great,

clumsy, flat-bottomed boat with one end rising up in a high keel. The other end remained open, waiting for passengers.

Jacob had already slid off his camel, assuming the particular, solid stance of a man bargaining. A boatman faced him. Leah knew that Jacob planned to pay extra silver and gold for the boatmen to work through the night. In record time they reached an agreement.

Now Leah watched while the camel drivers tried to coax the stubborn animals onto the boat. The experienced boatmen knew how. Pushing, beating, and kicking, they finally filled the ferry with six snorting camels. The drivers jumped onto the deck and commanded the camels to lie down. With long poles the boatmen shoved the craft away from the muddy bank.

"Gather all the children," Jacob told Leah. "You and Rachel and the maids will go next."

Three more frightened camels shared the boat for the second trip. Leah held Dinah tightly. She closed her eyes and prayed, "Take care of us, Lord."

"Don't be afraid, Mama," Judah said. "We can't sink. They have goatskins inflated with air tied to the sides of the boat to keep it from sinking."

At that moment the boat lurched and swung around so it faced the opposite shore. Leah clutched her daughter. "Sit down, boys, so you don't fall into the river," she shouted.

"It's all right, Mama," Reuben answered. "The boatmen told me that they use their long poles to push us into a current that swirls around here. The river will take us right where we want to land."

Glancing at the whirlpools and eddies in the water, she closed her eyes and prayed again.

Once off the boat, Leah followed the riverbank a short distance. She wanted to look across the water at the land she was leaving. Rachel followed and stood beside her.

"I wonder if Father will come after us and order us to return home with him," Leah said.

"He can't make us go home with him," her sister answered.

"How can you be so sure? Imagine how angry he must have been when he found out that Jacob had taken us away. He didn't agree to let us go, and he has never given us to Jacob."

"If Jacob had Father's household gods," Rachel said calmly, "he could inherit all of Father's possessions, including us."

Leah stared at her sister in stunned silence. Then she

whispered, "You have them. You took Father's gods. That's what you carried in the heavy bag when we left the house. Rachel! How could you steal them?"

"I brought them because I was afraid." Rachel drew in a sharp breath. "I'm still afraid Father will come and order us to return home with him. If we have them, Jacob can keep us. Otherwise, if Father ordered us home, Jacob could take Bilhah and Zilpah and go off to Canaan without us."

"Would Jacob leave you? He might leave me, but he wouldn't leave you, would he?"

"I didn't want to take any chances, and now we don't have to worry. I have the gods for Jacob to use if necessary."

"I don't like it," Leah muttered. "I don't like it at all."

Chapter 16

Throughout the night, all the next day, and into the following night the clumsy ferryboat drifted back and forth across the river. Before sunrise, when streaks of gold began to appear above the horizon, Jacob led his flocks and his people away from the rich, red soil of the Euphrates Valley.

Leah glanced back one final time at the river. All she could see was a row of date palm trees bordering the Euphrates, silhouetted against the morning sky.

She faced southward again. The desert plain stretched to the horizon, dotted with stunted tufts of rough, gray-green grass and scrubby dry bushes.

The head of her camel swayed in front of her. The muffled beat of hooves on the sandy soil surrounded her. Leah wrapped her shawl more firmly across her face to protect it from the cold bite of the wind. Behind her Dinah clung tightly, huddling under the back of her mother's shawl for protection against the bitter morning cold.

The sky reddened, turning the desert sand from yellow to pink, and then the sun rose in a blaze of red and orange. Daylight came rapidly and with it blue sky, cloudless and hard. And heat. By midmorning Leah's shawl became a protection for herself and Dinah against the harsh sunlight that beat down upon them.

Even with the dull sounds of the moving flocks and the incessant, low tinkling of camel bells, a strange quietness filled the desert. The voices of the children and the shepherds fell flat and dead with no hills to provide an echo.

The vastness weighed upon Leah. Could the Lord dwell here also in this flat land—this land with no mountains to rise up and inspire a feeling of His might and majesty?

The flocks advanced slowly, wanting to graze on the tufts of bunch grass and tear off twigs from the shrubs. The shepherds and dogs allowed some grazing and then drove them along until late afternoon when the fierce rays of the sun started to fade.

"Ai! Ai!" A shout of joy went up from the leading shepherds. They had sighted a pile of stones marking a well in the desert.

The sheep and goats spread out to graze. Released of their loads, the donkeys rolled over on their backs in the dust.

Leah and Dinah slid off their kneeling camel. Immediately it harshly announced its hunger. A camel driver removed the saddle and baggage and led it away to graze.

The women pitched the tents, then with baskets on their backs, searched along the caravan track for fuel—dry camel dung left from the many previous caravans that had passed that way.

Soon Leah had her cooking fire kindled. Catching a short-haired goat, she crouched to milk it. Suddenly a weird howl sent a chill up her spine. She stopped milking and called to Zilpah, "That's not a wolf. What is it?" The eerie sound came again and a chorus joined it.

"Jackals!" The servant woman replied. "They howl before they start to hunt. I remember their crying and barking. I heard it years ago when the caravan brought me up from Egypt."

"Where's Dinah?" Leah asked, looking anxiously around.

"I see her dashing into your tent."

Leah carried her large bowl of milk to the tent. Sobbing uncontrollably, Dinah sat by the back wall. Leah knelt and took her into her arms.

"What is it, child?"

"I heard that awful noise, and that's not all. Some bugs got in my eyes. They got stuck there, and I had to pull them away."

"They're desert flies." Leah kept her voice as calm as she could. "Here, let me wash your eyes with some milk." She poured milk from the bowl into the cup of her hand and splashed it into Dinah's eyes. "There, that should soothe the soreness away."

"Mama, I don't like it here. I want to go back home."

"So do I, so do I," Leah murmured. Her thoughts turned to her father. What was he doing? How had he reacted when he discovered that they were gone?

Jacob came to Leah's fire for the evening meal. To ward off

the penetrating night cold, he pulled his sheepskin coat closely around himself. With a tired sigh he said wearily, "I need you to get Rachel and the maids and the children. Before I eat, we must give thanks to the Lord."

She hurried to call them. Soon they stood together in a group, Jacob surveying the clear heavens and the first stars of the night. Leah and the others followed his example. They tilted back their heads to gaze upward.

"Lord, God of my father Isaac and my grandfather Abraham," Jacob prayed. "I praise You for bringing us safely this far on our journey to Canaan. I—my sons—my whole family praises You. Lord, You are our only God, and we are your people forever."

Leah tried to cling to the assurance that the Lord was with them in this flat, desert place, but it fled; and a suffocating worry spread through her mind. Rachel had stolen their father's household gods. Unknown to Jacob, the figurines traveled with them.

A jackal howled again. In response the sheep dogs growled and gave quick, sharp barks.

Later Leah lay in her tent, still wakeful even after the strenuous day. She heard the breathing of her three youngest sons and Dinah. Reuben, Simeon, and Levi were now old enough to sleep in Jacob's tent. A sheep dog growled outside at some small, nocturnal rodent. Shepherds hurled rocks from their slingshots at a marauding animal. A breeze brought the smell of fresh sheep dung—a warm, not unpleasant odor like a combination of grass and milk and wool. It reminded her of the security of home pastureland.

In the early morning darkness she got up to prepare for the day's journey. The caravan started on its way before the sun rose.

A west wind added blowing sand to the dust already enveloping the animals. The sheep plodded along, each sheltering its eyes in the coat of the one before it, trusting to the shepherds that only the lead sheep could see. The shepherds kept them moving, watching for any faltering that might result in a pileup and cause large numbers to smother.

A merchant caravan traveling from the south was little more than shadowy figures passing them in the dust.

In the late afternoon the wind died. Jacob halted his caravan in a shallow valley fringed with vegetation. Tufts of withered yellow grass held a few spears of spring green.

Leah pounded her tent pegs into the valley's gravely soil. The donkey that carried her tent had developed a sore on its back, and she treated it with comfrey salve. With no large stones to heat for baking bread, she let her fire burn into bright coals. Pushing them aside, she placed the thin disks of dough directly onto the hot earth. In a copper pan she parched wheat for the next morning's meal.

Drawing her hand across her eyes, she tried to wave away the heavy, acrid smoke from the camel dung. The smoke stung and smarted and obscured her vision. When she stepped away from the fire, a great brown vulture circled overhead. The last rays of sunshine caught on its widespread wings. A pack of jackals saw the fire and set up a series of barks and howls. Leah could imagine them after dark, prowling stealthily, ready for the kill.

Before she fell exhausted onto her sheepskins for the night's rest, she wondered how many days would pass before they could leave the desert behind.

A few days later rounded hills appeared in the distance. By evening Leah could pitch her tent near a clear stream that flowed from the eastern mountains. She carried sheepskins into the tent.

"Mistress," Zilpah called to her, "camels are approaching."

"Is it another caravan going north to Haran?"

"It's from the north." Zilpah's voice rose in excitement. "Mistress Rachel says it's your father and your brothers."

"Father! No! No! What will he do to us? Where's Rachel?"

She ran to her sister's tent. Without waiting to ask for entrance, she rushed in "Rachel, Father is coming. Where are his gods? Hide them. Put them someplace where he won't find them."

Here sister stood, frozen in fear. Then she jerked out of her dazed condition and clung to Leah. "They're already hidden. I've kept them hidden from Jacob."

They stared out at the approaching caravan. The camels came with quiet, measured steps. Soon Leah could hear their bells. The tall man on the lead animal was surely her father.

"I see Kesad and Jabal riding with Father," Rachel said.

Leah helped her to sit on a camel saddle, then slipped back to her own tent.

Jacob waited in front of his tent. Laban halted his camel as close as possible and stared down in silence at his son-in-law. Finally he ordered the camel to kneel. Getting off and with his hand on his beard, he confronted Jacob. Kesad and Jabal leaped off their camels and stood behind him.

"Get closer, Zilpah," Leah whispered, "and listen to what they are saying."

Anger filled the men's voices. The rest of the camp was still, hushed, suspended in apprehension. Dinah slipped into the tent and hid her face in her mother's lap.

"Will Grandfather take us back home?" she asked, her words muffled.

"I don't know."

"Will Father go away without us?"

Before Leah could answer, Zilpah rushed into the tent.

"What are they saying?" Leah asked.

"Master Laban says someone stole his household gods, and Master Jacob told him no one would do that. He offered to let Master Laban search all the tents. Whoever has the gods will be put to death."

"Mama." Dinah started to cry. "I'm afraid."

"Hush, child." Leah pulled her onto her lap and instinctively rocked her. Fear clutched Leah with icy fingers. *Whoever has the gods will be put to death. Rachel!* If their father found the figurines, her sister would die.

And then her father loomed at the entrance to her own tent and pushed open the flap. Silently, he poked at pillows and sheepskins. He peered into baskets. Then he was gone.

Leah peered out and saw him enter Rachel's tent. Panic gripped her. *Rachel, you should never have stolen Father's gods,* she moaned inwardly. *And Jacob why did you offer death?*

Her father remained a long time in Rachel's tent. Dinah clung to Leah's legs. Leah waited, peeking out the side of her tent. She knelt and put her arms around the little girl. Death for Rachel—Rachel, the sister she had raised like a daughter. Would Jacob really order death? A man couldn't go back on his word.

At last Rachel's tent flap slipped aside and Laban came out. He walked slowly to Leah. The late-afternoon sun glanced across his head. How old he looked! She had failed to notice until this moment that his beard was more white than gray.

Dinah let go of her mother and scurried into a back corner of the tent.

Leah stepped forward to meet her father.

"I'll search no longer for my gods," he spoke heavily. "I have no desire to see someone die, especially someone from my own family." With effort she kept her gaze from straying toward Rachel's tent. *He knows! He knows that Rachel has the idols.*

"I always take care of family," he continued. "Haven't I taught you to do the same? You know you must always respect your father." He paused briefly, then, "Now I'm ordering you to come home and manage my household. I have my wife, but she's no good at dealing with the slaves and bargaining with the merchants. I need you, Leah, and I want Dinah, too. I have enough sons, but I need my granddaughter."

Leah stared at him in amazement. The possibility that she could go home was breathtaking to her.

Laban gave a deep sigh and now he stumbled over the words. "I've—I've lost my household gods. Must I lose all my daughters and grandchildren also?"

"Home," Leah breathed. Here was her opportunity to return home. It would be easy and natural to say, "Yes, Father." If there were just some way she could go home and have both her father and her husband . . .

A cold sweat broke across her forehead, and her father became a blur in front of her. She must choose between him and Jacob. Her father . . . her husband . . . She wiped at her eyes with both hands. Her voice choked, "Father, I long to go home, but not without Jacob."

"Jacob doesn't love you. You know that. You know he wants only Rachel. He can have Rachel and he can have all the grandsons. I want just you and Dinah. Is that asking too much?" Laban stiffened and stared straight ahead. "You're my possessions, and I'm claiming you."

A wave of emotion swept over her. Never had she seen him display such feeling. He was a lonely old man, trying to hold on to what was important to him.

She must say something, but her sense of pain over his loneliness was too deep. It pulsated through her chest and into her throat, preventing her from speaking.

"My household gods are gone," her father continued sadly. "I'll never find them again. I can live without them. I can pray to Jacob's God. But I need you. Take down your tent, daughter, and pack your baskets. We're leaving."

With the greatest effort she looked directly at him. "No, Father, Dinah and I are not going with you."

"You would disobey me?" he shouted in astonishment. "You've never disobeyed me before."

Her voice rose clearly. "I'm not returning to Haran with you. I'm going to Canaan with Jacob."

"I could summon my servants and my sons and I could force you to go home with me. I'm your father and I have the right to take you and Dinah." His voice rang with the old authority that she knew so well.

But she had learned from him. She was his firstborn, much like him. Her voice too carried determination. "Dinah and I are not going."

"Bone of my bone," he said slowly, "and flesh of my flesh." A slight smile of admiration flickered around his lips as he studied her.

Then his body sagged. He was an old man again. "I will come to bid you goodbye in the morning." Turning, he walked to his camel.

She had humbled her father. The realization tore at her. She longed to ease his disappointment, and she wished she could care for him in his old age. Yet she knew she had made the right choice. Her heart throbbed as she thought of her love for Jacob—a love strong enough for her to refuse her father. If only she could tell Jacob that she loved him . . .

Stumbling into her tent, she sank in exhaustion onto a sheepskin. Barely had she touched the soft white wool when Rachel lifted the tent flap and rushed in. "I'm frightened," she said.

Leah sat up. "Here," she pointed at the sheepskin, "come sit with me."

Rachel leaned against her and sobbed. Leah put her arm around her sister. "Tell me why you're so afraid."

"I'm afraid to die. What if Father comes back and finds his gods in my tent? I'll have to die for taking them." She hid her face against her sister's shoulder. Her body was thin and frail under Leah's arm.

"Hush, Rachel. It's all right. Father knows you have the idols and he's not going to tell. He's giving them up to save your life."

"How can you be so sure he won't come back?"

"He may have deceived many people, but he has always been honest with me." She patted her sister and rocked her in her arms until Rachel's sobbing stopped.

"We have a strong father," Rachel said in a faint voice, "and you are more than a sister to me. You're my strong mother." She closed her eyes and with a tired sigh slumped onto the sheepskins.

Early the following morning Leah began the preparations for the day's travel. In a burst of gold the sun appeared in the east. From the hills Laban's small caravan marched toward the camp.

Apprehension began to worry away at her thoughts. Yesterday she had felt sure that her father accepted the loss of his gods and her refusal to return to Haran with him. Now would he confront her again? She watched him slowly approach her fire.

"I have come to kiss my daughters and my grandchildren goodbye." His voice shook.

"Get up, children," Leah called into the tent to Dinah and the three younger boys. "Your grandfather is here to tell you goodbye."

The children straggled out of the tent. Leah sent Issachar to Jacob's tent to bring the older boys. Laban kissed each grandchild, and they returned the kisses. Dinah clung to him, and he leaned down to stroke her hair. She lifted her face for his kiss.

Leah wanted to cling to him too. He had taught her the meaning of loyalty and obedience, of hard work and deep love.

Laban put his arms around her and she hugged him. "You're a good woman," he said.

"Thank you, Father."

"Take care of Rachel."

"I will. Yes, I'll take care of Rachel."

A brief pause at Rachel's tent, and then he was gone, walking stiffly back to his camels, riding north to Haran, the land that was his but no longer Leah's. She watched his caravan until it blurred in the distance.

She wasn't aware of Jacob until he stood beside her. "You disobeyed your father."

Leah bowed her head. "You heard me when Father was here yesterday?"

"I heard you and I was surprised. I never thought I'd live to see the day when you disobeyed your father."

She raised her head and looked at him. "He ordered me to go back home with him."

"And you refused. I don't understand you. You've always

136

been your father's daughter more than you've been my wife. You've always obeyed him faster than you've obeyed me. I've often wondered why you needed a husband to obey when you let your father dominate you. Now that you have the children you want, why do you need me?"

His sharp words shocked her, and Leah stepped backward. She had no idea he felt she didn't need him.

"Why do I need you?" She breathed out the words. "I need you because—because I love you."

There! She had said it after 20 years of yearning to tell him.

"You've never told me that before," he said quietly. Then his voice changed. "Pack your tent," he commanded. "Come, wife, it's time to move on."

Leah noticed a proud tone in his voice that she had never heard before, and for the first time he had addressed her as "wife."

For 20 years she had lacked the courage to tell him that she loved him. For 20 years she had tried to earn his love and acceptance.

As she turned away from the cloud of dust that was her father's caravan, an eagerness surged through her, a happy anticipation. She hurried to take down her tent to follow her husband to her new home, to follow him to the land of Canaan.

Epilogue

Genesis 49:29-31 records that when Jacob was old and ready to die, he charged his sons, "Bury me with my fathers in the cave that is in the field of Ephron the Hittite, in the cave that is in the field at Machpelah, to the east of Mamre, in the land of Canaan. . . . There they buried Abraham and Sarah his wife; there they buried Isaac and Rebekah his wife; and there I buried Leah . . ." (RSV).

About the Author

Beginning with Scripture's evaluation of Leah, Lois Erickson has used research, talent, and imagination to reconstruct the life of Jacob's first wife, making her a flesh-and-blood human being. She has also re-created the world of Haran in patriarchal times.

Visits to ancient markets in Istanbul, Dacca, and old Jerusalem gave her a new understanding of Leah's environment. Walking in the lower Himalayas of Kashmir, she observed shepherds taking their flocks to summer pasture. In Egypt she rode a camel.

Mrs. Erickson is the author of *Adventures in Solitude, Huldah,* and *Zipporah.* She has been published in such magazines as *Moody Monthly, Decision, Moments With God, These Times, Lutheran Digest,* and the Los Angeles *Times* travel section.

Lois Erickson and her husband, Ken, live in Eugene, Oregon, and have three children and seven grandchildren.

Also by Lois Erickson

Huldah
From the moment she disguised herself to sneak him to the Temple, Huldah seemed destined to play a leading role in young Josiah's life. Through the Assyrian capture of King Manasseh and the evil reign and assassination of Prince Amon, she had risked all to secretly teach him the will of God. But now that Josiah was ready to begin his perilous work, could she trust God enough to let him go?

Lois Erickson involves us in the intriguing story of a biblical prophetess and reveals how her dauntless courage resulted in the reign of one of Israel's greatest kings. Paper, 125 pages. US$7.95, Cdn$9.95.

Zipporah
She was a beautiful Midianite shepherdess. He was an Egyptian prince fleeing for his life. She resisted the attraction between them as if she already knew what it would cost her to love one of the greatest men in Hebrew history. A fascinating portrayal of the lives of Zipporah and Moses. Paper, 128 pages. US$7.95, Cdn$9.95.

To order, call 1-800-765-6955, or write to ABC Mailing Service, P.O. Box 1119, Hagerstown, MD 21741. Send check or money order. Enclose applicable sales tax and 15 percent (minimum US$2.50) for postage and handling. Prices and availability subject to change without notice. Add 7 percent GST in Canada.

Intriguing
Biblical
Narratives

Return to Jerusalem

The family thinks he is crazy. Grandfather Jared would risk his life by crossing 1,000 miles of hostile desert and mountains to resettle the devastated city of Jerusalem. But young Rachel understands. In fact, she wants to go with him. Together they brave danger from robber bands to reach the ancient city. There they are caught up in Nehemiah's struggle to rebuild the city and its walls. And there Rachel finds love. Author Lois Parker brings Bible history alive with bold, dynamic characters and the details of their ancient lifestyle. Paper, 128 pages. US$7.95, Cdn$9.95.

Song of Eve

In the tradition of C. S. Lewis, June Strong uses a story to portray the conflict between good and evil. The setting is before Noah's flood, in a world of garden-like beauty populated by men and women in the early glory of their creation. But this super race gradually forgets the God who made them.

Only a few people continue to sing a melody that Eve wrote after leaving the Garden of Eden—a song that mourns her great loss but promises a great hope. They move away from the selfishness and brutality of the cities and live in secret valleys. Will Shaina be able to leave her wealthy family and devoted fiancé to join those who sing the song of Eve and worship the Creator? Paper, 157 pages. US$1.75, Cdn$2.20.

Inspiring
Stories of God's
Healing Grace

April Showers
When Eric walks out on April, leaving her with three tiny children, tremendous bills, and no way to make a decent income, she doesn't have the slightest idea how to manage on her own. But as the months pass, her grief turns to anger, then action. Along the way she discovers a friend in her heavenly Father—and an unexpected romance. By VeraLee Wiggins. Paper, 125 pages. US$6.95, Cdn$8.70.

Because of Patty
When a phantom illness struck Sam and Mella's infant daughter, it should have been a tragedy. But their night of despair turned to joy because of Patty. This is a heartwarming story filled with a mother and father's anguish and dreams, sleepless nights, and tender moments with a little girl who always gave more than she took. By Paula Montgomery. Paper, 126 pages. US$7.95, Cdn$9.95.

Forsake Me Not
Devastated by a broken engagement and feeling betrayed by God, Megan leaves everything behind to try teaching in New York City. There she meets Mike, a youth pastor who helps her learn to trust again. Before long the couple fall in love. Then suddenly a violent wreck shatters their plans. Having learned that the Lord will never leave her, Megan pleads with God for help. His answer, while not what she expects, is beyond her wildest dreams. By Kay Rizzo. Paper, 156 pages. US$7.95, Cdn$9.95.

The Heart Remembers

A daughter, mother, and grandmother find themselves separated by a painful past. Yearning for acceptance, yet withholding forgiveness from each other as punishment, they realize their cherished grudges have locked them away from each other. This poignant story about forgiveness reveals how God's unconditional love can free us to let go of the pain and embrace each other. By Helen Godfrey Pyke. Paper, 108 pages. US$7.95, Cdn$9.95.

Jump the Wind

At age 14 the author stepped forward at an evangelistic meeting. Then her parents forbade her to attend the Seventh-day Adventist Church. Feeling cut off from the God she had just met, Sandra became involved with drugs and nearly ruined her life. This is the compelling story of how God reached out to her and calmed the storm in her life. By Sandra Bandy. Paper, 128 pages. US$7.95, Cdn$9.95.

Love's Bitter Victory

How do you tell your child you're sorry for missing the first 24 years of his life? Laura Michaels begins a journey away from alcoholism and discovers Jesus, a new start with her son, and a joy so contagious that it begins to change the broken lives around her. By Midge Nayler. Paper, 187 pages. US$8.95, Cdn$11.20.
